⌐ON LIBRARIES

D0591275

Valeron's Justice

Nash Valeron didn't expect starting up his doctor's practice would be so lively. But when a young woman arrives, his life is turned upside down and inside out. What begins as protecting the girl from a couple of bullies becomes a life or death situation. Land grabbing, murder and a host of killers are in Nash's immediate future. The only way to combat the odds is to ask for help from his family.

A lethal ambush, a corrupt asylum, and plots to kill the girl abound. And only the combined strength and savvy of the Valeron people can foil the wrongdoers' sinister plans. Who will be left standing after the blood and gun smoke finally clears?

Valeron's Justice

Terrell L. Bowers

A Black Horse Western

ROBERT HALE

ISBN 978-0-7198-2246-9

The Crowood Press
The Stable Block
Crowood Lane
Ramsbury
Marlborough
Wiltshire SN8 2HR

www.bhwesterns.com

Robert Hale is an imprint
of The Crowood Press

Typeset by
Derek Doyle & Associates, Shaw Heath
Printed and bound in Great Britain by
CPI Group (UK) Ltd, Croydon, CR0 4YY

CHAPTER ONE

Trina could not prevent the shiver that encompassed her entire body as the night guard paused at the open door, making his routine bed check. She prayed the darkened room hid the fact she was quaking under the thin blanket. Turk paused for a moment, likely hoping to see an exposed leg or shoulder from tossing in her sleep. The vision of him using the water bucket to douse her for the weekly bath caused bile to rise in her throat. The shame and abasement of being soaked while wearing only a thin dressing gown was almost more than she could bear. Then forced to wash her hair and be wet down again. . . . She gnashed her teeth to keep control of her emotions.

Finally, after what seemed hours – though it was more likely a few seconds – Turk lumbered down the hallway. This was his last round. She knew as much because of the clock in the dining room. It was visible from the hallway, and Trina had been keeping watch all night. It was time for Turk's relief. Manny Degorio and Jed (Turk) Turkleson took turns walking night guard and both were fairly predictable. She calculated she would have a minimum of fifteen minutes to make good her escape.

Having planned this for weeks, she already had the clothes she had managed to steal and hide under the thin pad that passed for a mattress. She had also learned to jimmy the door open to the hallway closet where the coats and shoes were stored.

Moving silently in her bare feet, Trina had already dressed under the covers and needed only a pair of shoes and a jacket or coat. She used the twisted piece of wire she had procured to jiggle the latch enough to open the closet door. Grabbing a pair of shoes, she wrapped them in a large coat, then closed the closet and scurried down the dark passageway to the rear of the building. The lone window in the washing room had a warped frame and the glass was too dirty to see through, but she had previously pried it open when no one was watching. It worked again and she shoved the coat bundle out. Scaling the short span of wall, Trina grunted and struggled to get through the opening herself. It was four feet to the ground, but she was able to lower herself without making any noise. She took a moment to re-close the window, slip on the ill-fitting shoes and much too-large coat. Then, straining to see where she was going, she hurried off into the early dawn, using the lingering darkness to conceal her movements.

The fence surrounding the Restful Acres establishment was six feet high, but she carefully scaled the wire to the top. She received a couple of scratches from the effort, but managed to reach the outside of the barrier. Taking a moment to get her bearings, she headed toward the nearby railroad tracks. She knew the train schedule and it was due at any minute, on its way to Denver and then Cheyenne. It always began to slow down as it passed by the asylum, so she was reasonably certain she could get aboard. With that feat behind her, she would hide out until she was safely through Denver. After that. . . .

Trina didn't think about the *after* part. She had lived and planned her escape ever since her incarceration. If she was caught, it meant being confined in a solitary room, possibly until she died. This was her one chance to get away, to run for her very life!

'You're really doing this?' Jared Valeron asked his younger sister. 'I mean, Nash has hung his shingle in a wild and untamed part of the country. Castle Point doesn't even have a sheriff. If they have need of a lawman, they have to request one be sent from Cheyenne.'

'So?' Wendy was undeterred.

'There are drovers, with rowdy cow punchers, pilgrims and settlers passing through, along with the occasional band of renegade Indians or bandits. You can also add in a passel of rustlers, drifters, hunters and trappers – all manner of undesirables.'

'You make it sound worse than Brimstone,' Wendy said wearily. 'Oh, but I guess that place doesn't count, since you and some of the others on the ranch tamed the whole outlaw town.'

7

'I'm not saying there aren't a few good people too, dear sister. I reckon there are some nearby farms and ranches, along with a handful of businesses in town. But it's a long way from the railroad, with nothing but a stage line passing through. It's certain to have a number of saloons, gambling joints and likely offers up every vice known to man. I doubt there isn't but a handful of decent womenfolk in the entire valley.'

Wendy feigned a yawn of boredom and passively replied, 'Then I guess there will be one more decent womenfolk when I arrive.'

'You'll be as out of place as a goat in a hen house.'

'Jerry, you're wasting your breath,' she stated with finality. 'I'm going to join Nash. That's the end of it.'

'You won't like the work,' he continued to challenge her notion. 'Do you even know what all a nurse is expected to do?'

'I think it's my calling,' Wendy piped back defensively. 'I'm a quick learner.'

'This is one of your daydreams doing the calling, sis. You never offered to tend any of the family when one of us were ailing, and I remember you passing out at the sight of blood!'

'Because it was my own blood!' she defended. 'And the kitchen knife did nearly cut off the end of my finger.'

'What about eligible men?' Jared tried a secondary approach to the debate. 'We've got a dozen or more single gents hereabouts, all of whom are panting at your heels like starving wolves after a crippled lamb.'

'Goodness, Jerry, such a charming picture of romance

you paint. I can't imagine how you've managed to stay single so long.'

He grinned. 'OK, so I'm about as tactful as a runaway freight train. But it's your future we're talking about.'

'What's all the cackling and squawking going on in here?' Locke asked, having been disturbed from doing some paperwork in his home office.

Both of them looked at their father, as he entered the room and regarded the pair with a frown. 'Jared, I thought you were helping Troy move a load of lumber today?'

'Naw,' Jared answered, giving a wave of his hand. 'He has Landau and Cliff with him. I would have gotten in the way.'

'He prefers to give me a hard time about leaving to join Nash,' Wendy informed him. 'I think he's worried that he won't have anyone to pick on if I leave.'

Their father sighed. 'We were all hoping Nash would set up his practice in town. However, the retired army surgeon who's doctoring there was the one who talked him into a career of medicine. There isn't work enough around here for two doctors.'

'Yeah, but Castle Point?' Jared grunted. 'Talk about a place between the badlands and the end of the civilized world.'

'Nash wrote to us about it,' Locke said. 'He claims the need for a real doctor is great in that part of the country, considering all of the travelers going through.'

Jared uttered a cynical laugh to make a point. 'Most of them pilgrims can't afford to pay a dime for treatment, Pa. I'll bet you're sending Nash money to live on within a month.' He jerked a thumb at his sister. 'And he sure isn't going to be able to afford a nurse!'

'Your mother and I have agreed to let Wendy go,' Locke ended the debate. 'However,' a sly grin came to his face, 'we had been discussing who we could send along to make certain she had a safe journey to Castle Point.'

'Not Jerry, Father!' Wendy wailed. 'Have pity on me . . . please!'

'I know,' he admitted, unable to control a self-satisfied grin. 'It's kind of like sending a weasel along to keep an eye on a ferret.'

Wendy scowled. 'I'm not sure I know the difference between those critters.'

'A ferret is smaller and equally as full of mischief, but it is a little bit cuter,' Jared quipped.

'Exactly,' Locke remarked jovially. 'Both of them have a nose for trouble.'

'I guess a trip to visit Nash wouldn't be so bad,' Jared said, thinking it over. 'None of the family have set eyes on him in months.'

'Yes, he was supposed to pay us a visit before hanging up his shingle, but his last letter said he needed to go as soon as possible. He didn't want another medico starting up a practice in Castle Point before he could get there.'

'And,' Wendy piped up quickly, 'he's sure to be overjoyed to have me as his nurse.'

Jared chuckled. 'Until a sick or injured person shows up. Then he might end up treating you for a fainting spell instead.'

'One time!' Wendy snapped defensively. 'I only got dizzy that one time—'

'All right,' Locke intervened to stop any more of their squabbling. 'I checked with Skip in town and he said the stage line in Cheyenne makes the several hour run to Castle Point every third day. If you leave in the morning, you should make the coach connection and arrive day after tomorrow.'

'I didn't know Castle Point was that far north,' Jared said. 'It must be almost to Fort Laramie.'

'It is. The Mormon Trail is close enough so the town services the travelers going through that part of the country, no matter which way they are headed.'

Jared looked at Wendy and sighed. 'Looks like me and you get to do some traveling together, sis. Better get your dainties and such packed.' He frowned. 'And I don't intend to haul a half dozen trunks around. You'll likely have plenty of time to sew yourself new clothes after you're there.'

'What I'd like to sew,' Wendy snipped, 'is your mouth – *closed*!'

Their father laughed. 'Wish I had the time to make the trip with you . . . just to referee your verbal battles!'

Dr Callisto stormed around the room, tossing his hands in the air, venting his wrath via oaths and curses. After the lengthy tantrum, he glared at the woman and two men who were responsible for security and order within the asylum.

'How did this happen?' he growled harshly. 'How *could* this happen?'

11

'She just vanished,' Turk muttered lamely. 'No sign of any door being forced. She was in her bed when I completed the last round. I watched her for a short while, making sure she was asleep.'

'Then she was gone when I went by doing the wake-ups,' Manny said. 'There was nothing out of place, the bed was just empty.'

Callisto looked at Zelda, the woman he called his nurse, although she was more like a female bouncer. She had wide shoulders and a blocky build, as strong as most men and with a face that would have better suited a bar room brawler. He asked her, 'What can you add?'

'A pair of shoes and coat have gone missing from the hall closet,' she answered. 'I couldn't find anything else.'

'Did you do a thorough search of the grounds?' he put the question back to his two men.

'She ain't here,' Turk said. 'We looked everywhere.'

Manny added, 'We did find some shoe prints over at the north side where she might have gone over the fence. If so, she probably headed for the train tracks.'

Callisto swore. 'That means she could have jumped on the train. She might be in Denver by now.'

'I believe the train only makes a short stop at Denver,' Turk said. 'Don't know that she has any friends there, and the police would hold her for us, being as she was ordered here for her mental condition. Her idea might be to stay on the train all the way to Cheyenne.'

'Every second she is free is a second closer to disaster,' Callisto told his employees. 'We can't have her finding help.'

'She's quite good looking,' Turk said. 'Most men tend to believe what a pretty woman tells them.'

'Get hold of those two bounty hunters, the ones we've used in the past. Tell them what we know and give them a description of the girl. We need her back – pronto!'

'I'll get my horse and round them up,' Turk replied. 'How much of a bounty are we offering?'

'Five hundred dollars, but they need to return her to us alive. It's imperative I get her back under my care before the court hearing. Once she is formally declared insane, we get our bonus from the client. After that . . .' He rolled his eyes. 'Well, the girl is pretty crazy. Who knows how she managed to get into the medicine cabinet. So tragic, but fatal accidents do occur sometimes.'

His features transformed into a dark and deadly frown, and his command was hedged with ice.

'Get her back!'

'Not to worry, boss,' Turk said. 'I'll find Pecos and Blocker and get them on her trail.'

As soon as he left the room, Callisto shook his head. 'Stupid hearing. If they had let us have our day in court last month, Miss Barrett would have been living in despair, without a spark of hope. If she gets someone to listen to her story, this could erupt into a bonfire.'

'How did she do it?' Zelda wanted to know. 'The medication has never failed to work. I gave it to her each day, the same as always.'

'She must have suckered you,' Callisto guessed. 'Probably spit out the liquid instead of swallowing it. Trina lulled us into not watching her close enough. I'll bet she has been planning this for some time.'

'When we get her back,' Zelda vowed, 'I'll damn well see that little witch swallows her medicine . . . or she will be sorry with every breath she takes!'

Trina managed a ride with a freighter, who was hauling a load of lumber north out of Cheyenne. He was an older gent with enough facial hair to pass for a mountain man after a long winter. Not a sociable type, he seldom spoke, but did give her a handful of jerky and let her drink from his water bag. It was the first food she had managed since her escape.

Along the slow, tedious ride, Trina kept watching the back trail. She had spotted two dirty, rough-looking men lurking like turkey buzzards when the train arrived in Cheyenne. They scrutinized every passenger who arrived at the station and examined each car. Fortunately, she had been hidden away within the undercarriage of the caboose and disembarked a half mile before the train came to a stop. She knew to avoid the railway inspectors who watched for free riders, as she had barely escaped detection at the Denver station.

After twelve hours of riding on the wagon, they spent the night at a way station. The teamster was nice enough to buy her a meal of stew for two-bits and she slept in the loft of the barn. They were moving again at daylight – before breakfast – and entered the edge of the small town of Castle Point at mid-morning. Trina thanked the teamster and thought her getaway successful until she caught sight of the same two men she'd seen in Cheyenne. Unfortunately, they saw her too!

Trina looked for a sheriff's office but there wasn't one. In desperation, she turned and ran down an alley, searching for somewhere to hide or a business or private residence that offered some protection. She had come too far to let them catch her now!

Wendy and Jared had located the small house with a *Nash Valeron, MD* shingle posted next to the front window. They entered through the door, which caused a small bell dangling on a string to ring. The two of them stopped to look around.

It was a bare room, except for a couch along one wall. Adjacent was a kitchen, with a table and four chairs, a counter beneath some cupboards and a small stove that provided for cooking and heating the diminutive house. Obviously, the treatment room was in the back, along with his bedroom.

'Doesn't look like there's any room for a live-in guest,' Jared summed up the situation, 'unless you sleep on the examining table. You're going to need a place to stay. Better hope Nash can afford to pay you wages.'

'Be right there!' Nash's familiar voice called from the next room. 'Give me five minutes or so.'

Wendy groaned, unable to hide her disappointment. 'I had hoped this was going to be more like a miniature hospital. You know, with several bedrooms and maybe an inside pump with water for a bath, that sort of thing.'

'Well, brother Nash is just getting started,' Jared cautioned. 'Maybe he can move to a bigger place once he starts making some money.'

'That boarding house we passed up the street looked

fairly new,' Wendy commented, giving her brother an imploring look.

'OK,' Jared said, knowing Wendy was already suffering from nervous apprehension. 'While you're waiting for Nash to finish with his patient, I'll walk up and check on it for you. If it looks good, I'll pick up your stuff at the stage office and move it to a room.'

'Thanks, Jerry,' Wendy said, smiling her appreciation. Then with an uncertain expression, 'I guess I'm in for a number of new experiences.'

He grinned. 'It's going to be tough, being out on your own for the first time.'

'Yes, the only time I ever stayed at a hotel was with the folks, except for one overnight shopping trip with Scarlet.'

'Time for the baby of the family to test her wings,' he jested. 'Just like a bird leaving the nest.'

Wendy firmed her resolve. 'You go ahead and get us rooms.' Then she hastened to ask, 'You are staying a couple of days, aren't you?'

'The return stage leaves every third day. I'll be around long enough for you to get settled . . .' he chuckled puckishly, 'and give you time to change your mind.'

She uttered a nervous laugh. 'I'm going to try and stick it out . . . for a while, at least. I don't want to quit without giving it my best effort.'

'All right. I'll be back in a few minutes.'

Soon as he left, Wendy moved through the house and took a peek into the treatment room. Other than the examination table and a couple of shelves with some medications and bandages, there was a small addition at the back of the house. It was a partially closed-in porch, and she also spied a tiny room to the other side of the house, just large enough for a patient's single cot, which took up most of the space. As for Nash's bedroom, it was off the kitchen and was very confined.

Wendy didn't wish to intrude while Nash was privately tending to a patient. He never noticed her watching, as he had his back to her and was wrapping up the leg of a middle-aged man. There was some blood on the floor and a nearby cloth was soaked with it.

Wendy gulped from the sight and backed away at once. There was something very unnerving about blood – especially human blood. She had helped to kill and pluck chickens, skin a rabbit or such, but this kind of—

The door burst open and a girl came rushing through the entrance way. Dressed like a back-street tramp, she was dirty and wild-eyed, with frazzled, unkempt hair, huffing and puffing from a hard run.

'Please!' she gasped, panting for breath. 'Hide me!'

Wendy recovered her surprise and offered her an uncertain smile. 'What's the matter, girl? Did you steal something? Or is there some love-starved gent on your tail?'

'Where's the doctor?' she wanted to know.

'He's treating a man in the next room,' Wendy replied.

'Are you the nurse?'

'Yes,' Wendy replied. Then, to correct the statement, 'I mean, that's why I'm here.'

'I need help,' she began to babble rapidly. 'I've been

17

held against my will for . . . I mean, I was ordered to be confined . . . imprisoned—'

'It's all right, dear,' Wendy tried to calm and reassure her. 'The doctor is with another patient in the other room. Just a minute.'

Wendy left her long enough to hurry to the back room. She poked her head inside.

'Nash!' she said to her brother. 'You've got another customer . . . uh, patient,' she amended.

He cocked his head enough to look over his shoulder at her. Smiling in his usual, assuasive fashion, he greeted her. 'Hey, little sister! It's good to see you.'

'Yeah, hi!'

'Is the patient bleeding or unconscious?'

Wendy told him she wasn't either of those things.

Nash was in the middle of removing the very bandage he had been putting on the patient. 'Stay with them until I finish. I didn't get enough pressure on the wound to completely stop the bleeding on the first attempt, so I have to put on a tighter dressing. Shouldn't be but a couple minutes.'

She gave a bob of her head, whirled about and rejoined the girl. 'Sit down, won't you?' she offered, tipping her head toward the waiting room couch.

The girl looked around nervously, but moved to the sofa and sat down. Before another word was said, two men came barging through the door. One was large, over six feet tall, plug-ugly, and had enough dirt and grime so that his complexion was nearly black. The man with him was shorter by several inches, slightly less offensive, but his bearded face, pointed nose, and pale, yellow-brown eyes reminded Wendy of a chicken hawk.

'What do you two men want?' Wendy asked, very uncomfortable in their presence.

The pair stopped and looked around the room. They saw the tattered female and eyed Wendy with a dismissive contempt.

'Don't you concern yourself with that there slippery female,' Plug-ugly growled, glaring straight at the newcomer. 'We'll shore 'nuff take her offa' your hands.'

'Yeah,' Chicken Hawk chimed his agreement. 'Stand aside, Squirt. She's our meat!'

CHAPTER TWO

Wendy shuddered inwardly, but took a deep breath to bolster her courage. She was a Valeron, and cowardice was not acceptable in their family. She faced the two men, mustered up a stalwart expression, and took a step to the side, placing herself between the two rowdy intruders and the raddled girl on the sofa.

'I'll thank you to leave this office,' she told the pair curtly. 'This young lady is waiting to see the doctor.'

Chicken Hawk jeered his contempt. 'She don't need no doctor, Squirt! Only a swift kick to the hind quarters afore we take her back where she belongs.'

'Who you calling Squirt?' Wendy flared back instantly, ire boosting her spirit. 'This girl is under my protection.'

'I don't think so. . . .' Plug-ugly extended an arm, poked her in the breastbone with an extended finger, and mockingly added, '*Squirt!*' a second time. Towering over her, he menacingly took a step closer.

'Listen, you,' Wendy warned him sternly, her anger elevated by their impertinence. 'I've got four older

20

brothers, and any one of them can kick your bucket! You touch me again and you'll have your hands chopped off and the fingers force-fed to you one at a time!'

He guffawed his scorn. 'You don't 'spect me to take you seriously, do you, Squirt?'

'You damn well should!' a harsh voice boomed from behind him.

Plug-ugly swung his head around.

A pistol barrel cracked him flush between the eyes, knocking him to his knees and raising an immediate vertical welt on his forehead. Before Chicken Hawk could react, the same gun muzzle was shoved up against his lower jaw, with the hammer cocked.

Jared drove him back until he was pinned against the nearest wall.

'Any man who lays a hand on my sister better darn well have her permission first, rat-face!' he snarled the words. 'You want to argue the point? Go ahead!' he hissed vehemently between gritted teeth. 'Give me a reason and I'll blow a hole through the top of your head and see how much sawdust comes out!'

The man's eyes bugged and he threw his arms high in immediate surrender. 'Don't shoot!' he cried.

'You got any last words?' Jared asked, his finger on the trigger.

'Uh, we sure as hell beg your pardon, mister,' the man blubbered rapidly. 'I believe there's been a mistake.'

'You made it!' Jared barked the words. Fixing him with a deadly stare, he challenged, 'If you've a mind to

21

have a go at me, I'll put my gun away and give you an even draw.'

The man violently shook his head in a negative motion. 'N-no, sir!' he stammered. 'We'll be taking our leave. Sure didn't mean to cause no commotion.' Then adding hastily, 'Excuse us – you and the young lady too!'

Jared stepped back, but kept the gun handy. 'Pick up your pal and drag his carcass outside. If he decides to take this a step further, I'll accommodate him. If he wants to see the doctor, he can wait his turn.'

'Yeah, OK, mister.' The bearded ruffian was agreeable. 'I'm sure my pard will be just fine, and no hard feelings. We sure didn't mean no disrespect to the lady.'

Jared watched as the man helped the dazed brute stagger out of the door. Once outside, he kicked it shut behind them and spun around on Wendy.

'What the Sam Hill, sis?' he wanted to know, holstering his pistol. 'I'm not gone ten minutes and you get us into a pickle with two of the town thugs!'

She was instantly defensive. 'I didn't do anything, Jerry. This girl' – she pointed at the haggard looking woman on the couch – 'she come in here looking for Nash. I don't know what those two wanted with her.'

'Where's Nash?'

'He's putting a bandage on a guy who mistook his leg for the chopping block with an ax.'

Before Jared could speak again, Nash entered the room. He was wearing a white smock and butcher's apron that had a smear of blood on it. He rinsed his hands in a pan of water on the kitchen counter, then dried his hands on a towel.

'Jer!' he greeted his brother warmly. 'Wendy didn't tell me you were with her.'

'You didn't give me time to say much of anything,' Wendy replied brusquely. 'And this gal on the couch probably isn't here to witness our family reunion. There's two ugly cusses chasing after her.'

Nash turned to look at the girl and asked, 'Miss? Can I help you?'

'I-I,' she began. 'I need to speak to you' – hesitantly – 'in private, if you don't mind.'

'Certainly,' Nash said, displaying a professional manner.

'What can I do to help?' Wendy asked.

'Jared,' Nash spoke to his brother, 'would you help Mr Tolkin to the door? He borrowed a cane to get here, so he can probably get home on his own.'

'Much obliged to you, Doctor,' the patient, Tolkin, said, hobbling out of the treatment room. 'I'll stop by to pay you soon as I get paid for my load of firewood.'

'Watch where you're swinging that axe and keep the dressing clean,' Nash warned. 'I'll want to look at it tomorrow.'

'Sure, Doc, whatever you say.'

Nash waited as the two men went out of the door then made a short appraisal of the malnourished and quite bedraggled woman.

'You look like you could use something to eat and a place to clean up.'

The girl ducked her head, ashamed for her pitiful condition. 'I've been caged like an animal for several months. I . . . I haven't eaten but one actual meal in three days, and that was a horrible stew and a piece of week-old bread.'

'Wendy,' Nash turned to his sister, 'take the young lady into the examination room. You'll see there is water, soap and towels. Let her clean up a little and I'll be in shortly.'

'But,' Wendy frowned, 'don't you want to know about her situation? I mean, those guys might come back.'

Nash smiled in a confident manner. 'Not while Jared is around, they won't.'

Without questioning him further, Wendy took the girl's arm and led her into the back of the combination doctor's office and living quarters.

Jared returned through the doorway to watch the two of them disappear into the back room. Once alone with him, Nash asked, 'What's the story about the girl?'

'I don't know. I didn't get a chance to talk to her. I happened along as Wendy was going toe-to-toe with that pair of ruffians.'

'From the girl's attire, she looks like a street beggar,' Nash observed. Then he turned to the other issue. 'What about those two men? I heard you threaten them from the next room. What did they want?'

'No idea, Nash, other than they were after the girl. One of them thought he could push our little sister around.'

'Yes, I did overhear the way you politely reprimanded them for using improper conduct with Wendy.'

Jared hunched his shoulders and let them fall back. 'You know how it is, Nash. I've always had something of a short fuse when it comes to one of the girls.'

Nash rubbed his hands together nervously. 'Jer, I have to live here. I hate to start off my practice with a reputation for pistol whipping someone in my office. I don't need that kind of publicity.'

'Once we find out why they are here, we can figure a way to deal with them,' Jared said. 'They must have followed the girl here for a reason.'

'Wendy can tend to her right now. We'll give her a few minutes and then have a talk with her. If she's on the run from the law or something, we might have to hand her over to the authorities.'

'Not to those two scumbags,' Jared vowed. 'They looked like hired toughs or bounty hunters.' He shook his head. 'If she's wanted by the law, I'll take her to Cheyenne and hand her over to the authorities.'

'Good thinking. We know she'd get a fair shake that way.'

Jared sniffed. 'Smells like something cooking on the stove. Me and Wendy haven't eaten since early this morning.'

'Fortunately, I was making enough chili to last me several days, when I stopped to bandage Tolkin's leg. Ought to be plenty for the four of us. We'll have a quick meal, then see what the girl has to say.'

'Sounds like a plan, Nash. Even your cooking sounds good right now.'

From a table and chair in the saloon, Pecos gave Blocker a good look. He clicked his tongue and bobbed his head up and down.

'It don't look too bad,' he made his diagnosis. 'Lucky

it didn't break your nose. You remember when I got hit by that buffalo hunter? Blacked both eyes and the swelling didn't go down for a week.'

Blocker started to frown, but grimaced at the pain such an expression caused. 'Who the hell was that guy?'

'Don't know, but he is shore 'nuff touchy about anyone giving his sister a hard time. I thought he was going to ventilate us both for a minute.'

'Callisto is going to be right unhappy if that gal spreads a story about him and finds some help. We need to get her away from that place.'

'Don't see how . . . not yet, anyway. That fella who hit you seemed like a man who'd ridden both sides of the fence. Either that, or he's just plain as quick with his temper as he is with a gun.' Pecos rolled his eyes. 'I've seen crazy wild and ice cold killers close up, and I got to say, that hombre was every bit as scary as any man I ever met.'

'Having a gun muzzle shoved up your nose makes a powerful impression,' Blocker said. 'Give me a couple hours to get rid of the blurred vision and ache in my head. Soon as I'm able, we'll figure a way to get the girl.'

'OK, pard,' Pecos said. 'I'll keep an eye on the doctor's place and see the girl don't leave. There ain't no sheriff in Castle Point, meaning we can do whatever we have to.'

Blocker gingerly fingered the welt running down his forehead. 'We can look for another way to get our runaway, but let's be sure we don't ruffle the feathers on that other gal. I'd as soon not provoke her brother a second time.'

'I'll go along with that,' Pecos agreed. 'Him, we'll give a wide berth to.'

Wendy helped the girl clean up and brush out the tangles from her hair. Then she loaned her a dressing robe and her spare night gown, so she didn't have to wear the clothes she'd worn for three days. Once presentable, and after eating her third helping of chili, Trina Barrett finally began to tell her story.

'My father owned a fair-sized ranch some twenty miles from Denver. My mother died when I was twelve and he remarried three years ago. The woman had a son who was a couple of years older than me.' She sighed. 'Lucile was sugar sweet and the perfect wife for the first few months, but her son used to run with an outlaw gang. He's nothing but a troublemaker and a bully, and his mother only wanted my father's money.

'Last year, my father died suddenly in his sleep. I stood to inherit the ranch because Dad had come to realize what kind of woman Lucile was. He had privately made out a will and stowed it safely in the hands of a Denver banker. But before I could assume control of the place and send Lucile and her son packing, they slipped something into my food or drink that made me terribly sick. A few days later, I woke up at a place called Restful Acres, a private asylum, run by an evil man named Callisto. He pretends to be a doctor, but he's a crook and a charlatan. The only thing he is good at is making people look sick or crazy.'

'You mean through the use of drugs of some kind?' Nash asked.

'Yes,' Trina answered. 'There are only a few patients, but they are all cast-off people – either from society or a wealthy party who wished to be rid of them. He charges a great deal to keep some of them confined there. I mean, how else could he afford a groundskeeper, cooks and maids, plus two full-time guards and a female overseer?'

'Such a large staff, for how many patients?' Jared asked.

'Five, including me.'

'Five?' Nash was stupefied. 'All those people overseeing only five patients?'

'One is a wealthy man, about sixty years old – his sons wanted his business; one is a discarded wife of a local banker – he has a new love interest; and there is a young pair of twins . . . the only ones paid for by the State.'

'And his treatment is some kind of drug?' Nash questioned her.

'Yes. He or Zelda – the woman overseer – gives each of us a daily dose of special medicine. Most of the time, me and the other inmates walk around in a daze. I can't speak for the others, but the world is full of strange visions, and ordinary conversation is impossible. It's like sleepwalking, but with the knowledge that you are awake.'

'Can you describe the taste or other symptoms?'

'Kind of bittersweet to the taste, usually one or two swallows. It always caused me to feel a hot flush and, when, or if I could speak, I was confused, irritable and short-tempered. It also gave me headaches and nightmares. As I said, some of those visions would take over my mind while I was wide awake.'

'It's called hallucinations,' Nash informed her. 'Did you have other effects, like cold clammy skin, stomach distress or a slowed down heartbeat?'

'I believe so – a little of all of those.'

'You know what the guy is using?' Jared questioned Nash.

'Several herbs or plants can cause similar symptoms – Jimsonweed, belladonna, or Lily of the Valley are a few that I learned about from a specialist in the field. All three of those can be fatal if used in a large enough dose.'

'You think your stepmother is paying the disreputable doctor to make you look unstable,' Wendy summed up Trina's situation. 'If you are declared insane, she and her son will assume legal ownership of the ranch.'

'There is supposed to be a hearing coming up,' Trina told them. 'I overheard the doctor and Lucile talking the day before I escaped.'

'The confinement at one of those places isn't the same as a prison, is it?' Jared again spoke to Nash. 'I mean, those two guys that came after her? Do they have a lawful right to take her back?'

'Only if the State recognizes the institution's right to keep a person against her will. With the twins being kept there, it would seem the sanatorium is sanctioned.'

'We can deal with that problem, can't we?' Wendy asked.

'I say we put Miss Barrett in a safe place, where she can be protected by an honest lawman until the hearing,' Jared recommended.

'We would still need to discredit the doctor to win her freedom,' Nash said. 'When it comes to proving a person's sanity, it's common for a judge to trust a doctor's diagnosis over the defensive claims the patient might make.'

'Then we need to get proof that the doctor's a charlatan,' Wendy proposed eagerly. 'I'll bet cousin Martin could figure a way to help us. He's studied law.'

'Only as a sideline,' Jared cautioned. 'His expertise is mostly finances and accounting, so he could manage the ranch and the businesses we own or oversee.'

'Besides, we would have to get samples of the medications the doctor is using,' Nash explained. 'Then we would need someone who could figure what and how they were controlling the patients.'

'You're a doctor, Nash,' Wendy said. 'You could handle that.'

'It isn't my field of medicine,' he replied. 'What we would need is a specialist, a chemist or pharmacist, one who. . . .'

At his brother's untimely, and lengthy, pause, Jared put a finger up in front of his lips. 'Sh-h-h,' he whispered to the two girls, 'I believe Nash is trying to conjure up a genuine thought.'

Nash laughed at the heckling. 'You haven't changed a bit, Jer – still picking on the youngest boy in the family.'

Jared grinned. 'So, Dr Amazing, tell us what bright idea you came up with.'

'A research pharmacist named Dizzy Delacruz. I

worked with him some when I was doing my apprenticeship at the hospital in Denver. He's the one who gave me the info on how much chloral hydrate to mix into the whiskey bottles when you and Brett were in Brimstone. He's a trifle on the odd side, but a walking text book on medicinal plants and poisons.'

'That's handy, him being so close to our destination.'

'But,' Trina finally entered the conversation, 'wouldn't you need an order from a judge or something to seize Callisto's compounds for testing?'

Jared shrugged. 'Give us time to figure a plan, Miss Barrett. There are other ways to get what we need.'

'First thing,' Wendy pointed out, 'we have to deal with the two goons who came after Trina.'

Jared flashed a meaningful wink at Nash. 'You know, little brother, I feel a little bit guilty for clubbing that one bruiser like I did. I really ought to try smoothing things over with them. Who knows? They might be reasonable fellows.'

'Reasonable!' Wendy exclaimed. 'They are barbarians who—'

Nash smirked and she knew she had missed some covert exchange between her two brothers. Checking Jared's expression, it was evident he had a plan in mind. Nash had picked up on the idea and suggested, 'Maybe you ought to buy them a drink and see if you can make things right.'

'Exactly what I had in mind,' Jared agreed.

'I'm lost,' Trina put in lamely. 'Is your family always like this – weird, mysterious and communicating in some secret code?'

31

Wendy laughed. 'Yes, Trina, it's precisely how our family is.'

A full night's sleep in the patient's room, a good breakfast and a bath helped Trina look like a normal young lady. Wendy bought her a hairbrush, outfit and shoes at the general store so she no longer looked like a beggar. No one else came searching for her, so once presentable, she joined the three Valerons for a discussion about her future.

Nash and Jared each sat on one of the chairs from the dinner table, while Trina and Wendy relaxed on the waiting room sofa.

'What about the two men that were after me?' Trina started the conversation. 'I've been afraid they would return to take me away.'

Nash paused before speaking, momentarily distracted by the young woman's appearance. Decked out in a new dress, Trina was much more attractive than he had first thought. Her corn-silk colored hair was freshly brushed and the locks dangled loosely on either shoulder. Her eyes were alert and a dusky blue, like deep water in a crystal clear lake. With a petite nose and slender, sensuous lips, she would have made a proper sculpture's model. He recovered his senses and produced a crooked smile.

'They won't bother you again,' he assured her. 'Jer sent them home.'

Trina altered her attention to Jared. 'You *sent them home?*'

Nash's brother lifted his shoulder in an off-hand-variety of a shrug. 'I apologized to the pair for being overly aggressive with them,' he explained. 'Then we shared a bottle for an hour or so and darned if they didn't go to sleep on me.'

'Sleep?' she queried, still muddled by his actions.

'Yes, ma'am,' he replied. 'They were enjoying the snooze so much, I personally had to see them to the stage this morning. I don't think they'll be back.'

'The stage? I thought they came by horseback?'

He gave a second shrug. 'They were in no condition to ride.'

'I don't understand.'

Nash laughed and told her, 'They weren't conscious when they left town. Jared gave them some whiskey laced with chloral hydrate. I doubt they will wake up until they are all the way back to Cheyenne.'

Trina shook her head in amazement. 'But . . . why would you do that for me? You don't know anything about me.'

'We believed what you said,' Wendy was the one to reply. 'If a crooked doctor is controlling you with some kind of drug, we're going to do something about it.'

'When is this hearing and what exactly does it mean?' Nash wanted to know.

'I think it is to be around the first of the month. If I don't show up, the judge could rule that my father's will does not apply. Dr Callisto will testify that I am not mentally capable of looking after myself, let alone run a cattle ranch. I could lose everything and be labeled insane.'

'Then we have to get things in order before the

hearing,' Jared proclaimed. Turning to Nash, 'We need some samples of those medications for your pal, Dizzy. We get the goods on the doctor, the rest will be easy.'

'It might be dangerous,' Nash said.

'More dangerous than you might think,' Trina warned them. 'I told you about Robby, my stepmother's son. He used to ride with a notorious outlaw band, and has been in and out of trouble with the law most of his life. He lost his temper with me one time and threatened to cut my throat with a knife! I'm certain he wouldn't hesitate to do it.'

'I'll try and bring up that little episode, when I meet him,' Jared said, the muscles tight around his jaw. 'I don't hold with anyone threatening or mistreating a woman.'

Trina bobbed her head. 'After seeing how you manhandled those two men yesterday, I don't doubt your word one bit.'

'Jerry has always been a very protective big brother,' Wendy said with some pride. Then showing her pixie simper, 'Just don't ever agree to play *Rescue* with him.'

'Do what?' Trina asked. 'What is *Rescue*?'

'A game we boys used to play,' Nash advised her. 'Usually Jared and me against Brett and Reese, if it was only our family.'

'Yes,' Wendy snipped, 'with me as the victory flag.'

Trina frowned. 'I don't understand.'

'We pitted one older and one younger Valeron boy against the other two,' Nash explained. 'Wendy, being the youngest girl in our family, was usually the damsel in distress.'

'It's the only way they would let me play with them,'

34

Wendy complained. 'I never got a wooden gun or knife, because I was a girl.'

'I gave you a gun once,' Jared corrected. 'Remember?'

'Oh, sure,' she said, pulling a face. 'You call that little thing you whittled a gun?'

'It was supposed to be a hideaway gun, like a Derringer,' Jared said. 'Isn't my fault if you lost it.'

Wendy scowled at him. 'I didn't lose it, the stupid thing wouldn't stay in the waistband of the trousers you loaned me to wear. It slipped down and came out one of the leg holes!'

They all laughed, and then Nash continued with the rules of the game.

'Brett and Reese would take Wendy out into the hills or nearby woods and use her as bait to trap or catch us. Our job was to rescue her without getting caught.' He grunted. 'I got caught or killed every single time, but they never got Jer.'

'And I sometimes was tied to a tree or kept prisoner for hours at a time,' Wendy complained. 'Jerry would usually find a way to get me free' – she giggled and pointed at Nash – 'often by using poor Nash as a diversion.'

'I was no good at sneaking around in the woods,' Nash admitted. 'But Jer was like a whisper of a breeze. He moved without sound and could hide behind a single blade of grass.'

'So Jared always set you free?' Trina asked Wendy.

'Free?' Her voice was shrill. 'One time he threw a rope over me and dragged me off behind his horse! If I had lost my balance, I'd have also lost all of the hide off my elbows and knees!'

'Hey, I was saving your life,' Jared excused his actions. 'Besides,' he grinned, 'you always could run faster than either Reese and Brett.'

The four of them all laughed for the second time – the three Valerons at the memory and Trina at the visual imagery the tale brought to her mind's eye.

Nash lifted a hand to return to the serious problem at hand. 'We're not playing a game this time, big brother. I think we better expect more trouble.'

'And you'd better not figure me for being as fast afoot as Wendy,' Trina warned. 'I've never worn men's trousers, but it's a real chore to hold up petticoats and get any speed up while wearing a dress.'

Jared had already been doing some planning. 'First thing, we're going to wire the courthouse and get the exact date of the hearing. When it comes time to make the trip to Denver, we will make the plans very public.'

'You mean invite an attack,' Nash deduced his plan.

'Always better to know what you're up against. If we let them pick the time and place, it could mean real trouble. If we control that much, we have the upper hand.'

'How much money does your stepmother have to work with?' Nash asked Trina. 'Can she afford to hire several gunmen?'

'We have about 500 cattle, a remuda of fifty or so horses, and a pretty decent ranch house and out-buildings. Our four full-time hired hands take care of everything except for the roundup. We also have a yard man for tending animals and such. Besides them, we use temporary help.'

'Sounds as if Robby has access to enough money to try and prevent Trina from getting to the courthouse,' Wendy said. 'With her no longer under the doctor's care, they might hire several men to stop her from making it to the hearing.'

'I agree,' Nash said. 'Jer, you might want to line up some help for our side.'

Jared grinned. 'Way ahead of you, little brother, way ahead of you.'

CHAPTER THREE

Lucile Gowan-Barrett sat across from Dr Callisto's desk, with arms folded and glaring eyes scalding the doctor. 'I'm paying you a fortune to do one little chore and you let that sassy little wildcat escape?'

'I've sent a pair of competent bounty hunters to track her down,' Callisto ensured her easily, as if there was nothing to worry about. 'I expect they will have her back at any time.'

'The hearing is in two weeks!'

A second complacent look. 'Not to worry, Lucile. One treatment is all it takes. I promise you, the girl will flounder like a fish out of water. She will be too incoherent and disoriented to defend herself.'

'What about afterward?'

'As we previously agreed, I will maintain her care until the court hearing determines she is not competent. Once she is no longer a threat to you or your ownership of the ranch, we can release her, or you can continue to pay a fee for housing her here with us. A third option would be if you wished to assign her to another facility where they can look after her.'

Manny entered the room without knocking. The facility guard had a look of consternation on his face. 'Uh, boss,' he muttered almost inaudibly, 'them two hunters you hired are here to see you.'

'Aha!' he exclaimed triumphantly. 'What did I tell you, Lucile?'

'It's just the two of them,' Manny clarified quickly. 'They come alone.'

'What!'

'They are waiting in the entrance hall.'

Disregarding Lucile, Callisto strode smartly out of the room and hurried to the visitor's area at the front of the building. Blocker and Pecos both had their hats in their hands, appearing shame-faced, with eyes lowered and bowed heads.

'What happened?' Callisto demanded. 'Where's the girl?'

'She's up at Castle Point,' Pecos informed him.

'Castle Point! Why isn't she here with you?'

The two men looked at each other before Blocker commenced to speak. 'You see, Doc, there was this guy—'

'He's the one who put that nasty bruise on Blocker's forehead,' Pecos interjected.

'Yeah,' Blocker continued. 'He done that 'cause I poked his sister with my finger.'

Callisto uttered a confused, 'You did what?'

'The guy hit me when I wasn't expecting it,' Blocker complained.

'I couldn't do nothing, either,' Pecos said, failing to

add to the explanation of what either of them was talking about. 'He had me under his gun soon as he hit Blocker. He was like an angry bull, goring everything in sight.'

'Tell me about the girl!' Callisto almost yelled.

'She was there,' Pecos told him. 'We would have had her too, if not for that fellow butting in.'

'Why didn't you stick around and grab her later?'

'Come to find out, the guy who nailed Blocker with his gun barrel was a Valeron,' Pecos said. 'He come round to visit a couple hours after our little scrap. He brung us a bottle of whiskey – said it was a peace offering for getting rough.'

'We warn't looking for no trouble with the Valeron clan,' Blocker chipped in. 'So we tossed back a few drinks with him.' He added quickly, 'We thought he might be reasonable about letting us have the girl.'

'So, what happened?'

Blocker lifted and dropped his shoulders and Pecos uttered a deep sigh.

'What happened?!' Callisto shouted the question a second time.

'Dunno,' Blocker squeaked in a meek voice. 'We woke up about the time we arrived back in Cheyenne . . . on the stagecoach.'

'Must have been something in the drink,' Pecos speculated. 'We had our lamps doused for a solid twelve hours. We come to and had $100 each in our pockets – payment for our horses. The rest of our gear was in the boot of the coach.'

'Why the hell did you come back here?' Callisto

cried. 'Are you gonna let some wandering interloper get away with doing that to you?'

The two men's attitude changed, but not to flinch from his wrath.

'Do you have any idea who the Valerons are?' asked Blocker.

'We ain't gonna cross one of them!' Pecos echoed his concern. 'No one in his right mind tangles with a Valeron.'

'I never heard the name of Valeron!' Callisto fired back.

'There's your answer,' Blocker suggested smartly, though it made no sense to the doctor. He explained, 'Find someone to do this here chore who never heard of them.' He narrowed his gaze. 'Just be sure it's someone who won't admit to anyone as to who sent them to do the job. Rile one of the Valeron clan and they will hunt you to the ends of the earth.'

'And there ain't no place you can hide from them,' Pecos replicated his partner's words.

Callisto swore. 'Of all the gutless, yellow—'

'We only come by to warn you,' Pecos cut off the doctor's criticism. 'There ain't enough money in the whole State to pay us to lock horns with a Valeron. We're pulling out of this here job . . . and this part of the country.'

'Best heed our warning,' Blocker said. 'You mess with the Valerons and it'll be your end.' Then he and Pecos whirled about and went out of the front door.

Callisto could not close his mouth, so completely dumbfounded was he by the reaction and overt

41

cowardice of the two bounty hunters. He had thought them willing to do anything for the right price. Obviously, he'd misjudged them terribly.

With a storm cloud of dread hanging over his head, he plodded back to the room where Lucile was waiting. Her impatience was engraved on her stone face as her smoldering eyes seared his hide.

'Well?' she bit off the word sharply. 'Where's Trina?'

Callisto shook his head. 'At this moment, she is up at a place called Castle Point.' He explained how the two bounty hunters had been duped into returning without her.

'You told me there was nothing to worry about!' she reminded him hotly.

'It seems the girl has gotten some help,' he replied. 'Have you ever heard the name Valeron?'

'I believe it's a border town a hundred or so miles from here. My son, Robby, told me about riding through it one time.'

'Well, there is a family by the same name up that way too. Evidently, they have a habit of sticking their noses into other people's affairs. The two men I hired are afraid to go up against any member of their family.'

'That's ridiculous!'

Callisto wrung his hands nervously. 'The thing is, Lucile, I don't know anyone else to hire for the job. Those two hunters have always been willing to bring in a new patient or one who happened to escape.'

The woman scowled, but her furrowed brow gave evidence she was measuring options. When she spoke, it was with conviction and a grim satisfaction.

'All right,' she said thickly. 'We tried to do this so that pasty-faced vixen didn't get hurt. Now we'll do it the only way left open to us. Robby used to ride with some unsavory characters. One of them has his own gang, they're part Mexican, part Indian, and all ruthless outlaws. Robby can sic them on the girl and this scary protector called Valeron. They will put an end to all of our troubles.'

'I gave you the compound you needed to be rid of your husband, but I want nothing to do with any more murders,' Callisto told her firmly.

'None of this should even be necessary!' she snapped. 'My husband, James, must have guessed our plan to get the ranch. The conniving, underhanded cuss wrote a will and left me and my son with nothing. It's on his head that I'm forced to get rid of his daughter.'

Callisto displayed not the slightest empathy. 'I just want it clear – if you hire people to be rid of Trina, any repercussions are on you and your son.'

'Yeah, yeah, I understand.' She uttered an unladylike oath. 'You don't mind stealing these people's lives and making them slaves to your potions, but you are above killing them.'

Instead of affront, the doctor responded, 'That's exactly right.'

Nash discovered Trina to be a hard worker. She insisted on cooking and cleaning, and helped with organizing his medications and equipment. Wendy even complained how the young woman's ambition left little for her to do. However, working together provided the two girls with a chance to get to know one another and they became fast friends. Nash was often left out of their conversation because much of it was fashion or recipes or similar female subjects.

A week passed, with Wendy staying at the boarding house, Jared at the hotel, and Trina sleeping in the patient room. Then, one early afternoon, there came a crisis. Nash and Trina were busy doing an inventory of his medical supplies, bandages, while Wendy was busy sweeping the rest of the house. That's when the front door burst open. A sizable man had a slender young girl in his arms and a very worried woman rushed ahead of them.

'It's our daughter!' she cried out to Wendy. 'She's running a fever and has been growing sicker for the past two days. The right side of her lower stomach area is swollen and extremely tender to the touch. You must help her!'

Nash came from the next room, having heard the commotion. 'Bring her through and place her on the examination table,' he directed the man, indicating the next room.

Trina quickly wiped her hands and, before the man arrived with the girl, she had smoothed the sheet that covered the tabletop.

The girl was no more than twelve years old, and her face was contorted and flushed from the combination of fever and pain. Wendy knew to remove the parents so Nash would have room to work on the young girl. By the time she had escorted them back to the waiting room, Nash had begun his examination.

'Have you lost your appetite lately?' he asked the girl. At her nod, he added, 'And you're suffering from nausea?' At her frown, he clarified, 'Vomiting?' Another grimace as she bobbed her head. 'And where did the pain start?'

'Kind of at my belly button,' she gasped, gritting her teeth from the terrible ache.

'And it's now here on your lower right abdomen – your right side?'

'Yes.' She sniffed, holding back tears. 'It hurts more'n anything I ever felt before.'

'It's her appendix,' Nash diagnosed. 'If it hasn't burst, it is very close to doing so.'

'One of our ranch hands died from that,' Trina recalled. 'By the time we got him to the fort surgeon, there was nothing the doctor could do.'

'No, when it ruptures, it spreads poison throughout the patient's system.'

'Can you stop it from bursting?' Trina asked uneasily.

'I've read about the procedure. It's brand new, but it was done with a degree of success a few months back. However, it is an operation I've never seen. The drawings were pretty vague, but I have examined a person's appendix before. I know where to look and what has to be done.'

Wendy came into the room. 'Did I hear right? You're going to operate?'

'If it is the appendix, it's her only chance to survive,' Nash said. 'Tell her parents while I get the instruments ready.'

'What can I do?' Trina asked.

'I'm going to need both of you to help. Think you are up to it?'

Trina stated unwaveringly, 'I've never been squeamish.'

'Will . . . will there be a lot of blood?' Wendy was more timorous. 'I mean, I'm not sure if I can. . . .'

Nash glanced at his sister. 'You will handle the chloroform. We'll need to keep the girl sedated, but we have to make sure not to use too much. I'll walk you through it.'

The girl whimpered from fright and the acute agony in her lower abdomen. 'Please,' she murmured. 'Please. Do anything. But make the pain stop.'

An hour later, the young girl was asleep in the patient bed where Trina had been spending her nights. Her mother was sitting with her, while her father was trying to barter something of worth to pay for Nash's handiwork.

'You understand,' Nash told him, 'it will be a couple of days before we know if there was any infection. The removal of the appendix went well, and there didn't seem to be any leakage when I tied it off, but it is a surgical procedure I've never seen before. If the fever abates and no new symptoms appear in the next three days, then we can all give a sigh of relief.'

'It's just that we are headed to Utah to join our family,' the man explained. 'I've spent every dime I have on the provisions and supplies to get us there. If there's some work I can do for you – I'm a carpenter by trade. Let me build something or make some repairs to repay you.'

'I would like to enclose the back porch for a second bedroom,' Nash suggested. 'It shouldn't take more than a day or two and I could pay you the difference.'

The man held up his hand. 'Say no more . . . and I'll still be in your debt.'

'Let's step out back and you can take a look at the porch. Then I'll tell the man at Joe's Lumber, Tools and Coal Yard to give you whatever you need.'

Wendy and Trina were finishing up with the laundering of the sheet and items that had been soiled from use during the operation. Once they were alone, Wendy thanked Trina for her help.

'I'm the one who owes you and Dr Valeron my thanks. You saved me from being taken by those two bounty hunters. If not for you, I would be medicated and back at that asylum by now, staring blankly at the walls and drooling down my chin.'

'You were great,' Wendy praised her. 'When Nash cut into that girl's flesh, I. . . .' She shuddered at the memory and wrung her hands. 'I don't know how I ever thought I could do this.'

'You did a very good job,' Trina argued. 'That little girl never once flinched or moved. You kept her in a deep sleep the whole time, yet Nash woke her when he had finished the stitches and bandage with no trouble at all.'

'Yes, but what if you hadn't been here to help? I couldn't have done what you did – helping sop up the blood and actually holding the wound open for—' Wendy stopped, unable to keep from gagging at the memory. She ducked her head and blinked at the tears

47

that entered her eyes from fighting down the swell of bile within her throat.

'See?' she gasped. 'I can't even talk about it!'

'Many people are affected by the sight of blood,' Trina said gently.

'Maybe,' Wendy grunted her disgust, 'but I'll bet not one of them is dumb enough to try and become a nurse!'

Robinson Gowan sat down in the dark corner of L.G. Meadows's trading post and tavern. Having sent a telegraph message, there was a man waiting for him. It was early afternoon, so the rest of the place was nearly empty. Breed – as he called himself, claiming the mixed blood of Spanish and Comanche blood – wore a combination of buckskin and denim, with riding boots and a wide, flat-crowned hat that partially hid his face. Dark of skin, he could pass as Indian or Mexican. His face was pinched, with high cheekbones and a slender nose. A natural sneer twisted his lips, partly due from a scar along one cheek that ran to his chin. He stuck out a hand in greeting, while his dark eyes glowed like smoldering embers in the dim tavern light.

'Thought I'd seen the last of you, Robby boy,' Breed said, pushing a hall-full glass of whiskey over in front of him. 'Figured you were done with any shady business, since your ma latched on to a prosperous ranch owner.'

'Hooked a big fish there,' Robby agreed, 'but there's a snag we need taken care of.'

'And you thought of your old pal, knowing I could free your line.'

Robby took a swallow of the cheap rot-gut and pulled a face. 'I'll pay you enough that you won't have to drink this cheap snake juice for a spell.'

Breed clicked his tongue. 'Well, you know the pickings are pretty lean, what with most of the Indians confined on reservations. We have to choose our targets with care.'

'Then you still done Injun garb for your attacks.' It was a statement. 'That's good.'

'It ain't like we don't actually belong to one of the tribes,' Breed said. 'Claw and Hawk are from the Sioux and Lobo is part Cheyenne.'

'How about Kidd and Mont?' Robby grinned. 'One's Irish and the other is German.'

Breed laughed. 'Adopted members of my special tribe of renegades, Robby, old son.'

'Any others?' Robby asked. 'This target might be protected by a couple riders. I don't want you taking on a job without adequate firepower.'

'I've used others from time to time, but that's providing the job pays enough to warrant the extra guns.'

'One thousand dollars in cash,' Robby offered.

Breed whistled softly. 'Must be a high-ranking government official or something.'

'It's the daughter of the rancher Ma married. The double-crossing old goat made out a will and left the place to her.'

Breed laughed. 'I told you not to move in with your mother. Being a family man don't suit the kind of lives we lead.'

'Can you handle the job?'

49

'You say the target is protected?'

'Some guy named Valeron. You ever hear of him or his family?'

'Seems we rode through a town near the Colorado-Wyoming border with that name.'

'Yeah, I was with you at the time.' Robby waved a careless hand. 'Come to find out, the town is named after the family who owns most of it.'

'Been through a few burgs like that before,' Breed said. 'I don't see it as a problem.'

'This Valeron joker is helping the girl. He is going to deliver her from Castle Point to Denver for the hearing on the ranch. It's scheduled for next week.'

'We don't hit trains, but we can maybe stop the stagecoach before it reaches Cheyenne.'

'Should be easier than that, Breed. I've learned they are traveling by buckboard or carriage from Castle Point to Cheyenne. Ought to be any number of places where they will be vulnerable to attack by a few *renegade Indians*.'

Breed thought about it for a moment. 'And you say there won't be but one or two men with this gal we're after?'

'I paid a handsome fee to get a look at the telegraph messages. They are going to meet the train in Cheyenne. However, the timing of their trip fell between the stage runs.' He handed him a piece of paper. 'Here is the timetable.'

'Kind of left this until the last minute, didn't you?'

'Two bounty hunters were supposed to grab the girl, but Valeron turned the tables on them. The cowards backed out on the job. They had shown their hand and didn't want to get their names on a wanted poster.'

'Hard to find trustworthy help these days,' Breed said.

'What do you say?' Robby asked. 'You'll have to act quickly because they are due to travel in a couple of days.'

'When do we get paid?'

'Half now,' Robby told him, pulling out a wad of bills, 'and half after the job is done. Just drop me a line where to meet you.'

'Right here, one week from today.'

'Done.' Robby gave him the money, shook his hand and left the table.

Breed watched him go, leaned back in his chair and began to count the money. Robby had never been a favorite member of his gang, but he had done his share. The boy was too tied to his mother's apron strings to cross from milksop to a hardened desperado, but the money sounded good.

Lobo had been watching from a dark corner of the room. Breed never talked business without someone having his back. Lobo had been with him since they formed their little band, as close to a brother as Breed had ever known.

'Looks like we got paid in advance,' Lobo approved, glancing at the money.

'You remember Robby?'

'It's been a while,' Lobo said. 'He's the one we used to call Mama's Boy behind his back. Been a couple of years since we've heard from him, ain't it?'

'Yeah, his mother's plan to score a big cattle ranch by marrying some guy hit a bump in the trail. We are supposed to remove that bump for them.'

'How big a bump we talking about?'

'Lobo, you best contact the Pratt brothers.' He skewed his expression in concern. 'Someone named Valeron might be involved.'

'Hope that ain't Wyatt Valeron,' Lobo said. 'I heard a story or two about him. He's supposed to be hell on the hoof with a gun.'

Breed snickered. 'If it's him, we won't give him a chance to use his speed. We are going to set up an ambush and kill every single person riding with that girl before they know what hit them.'

'So why give away a chunk of our cash to the Pratt boys?'

'Better to share a bit of the money and make certain of the raid, rather than take a chance and maybe get one or two of us killed.'

Lobo chuckled. 'Like I said, good thinking, Breed. I'll send word and have them here by tomorrow.'

CHAPTER FOUR

Martin Valeron arrived at Castle Point with two of the long-time employees from the ranch – Reb and Dodge. The two hands got a room at the hotel, while Martin conferred with Nash, Wendy and Trina.

Trina was impressed by Martin. Though he physically resembled the Valerons she had already met, he seemed cut from the same mold as Nash – a thinking man, not a fighting one like Jared. Upon learning of the drug-induced prisoners, he was incensed and vowed to take down the unscrupulous crook who was posing as a genuine doctor. It was decided that he and Wendy would leave immediately so they could catch the return stage to Cheyenne, while Reb and Dodge would remain to help Jared with his plan.

Trina prepared a meal of fried chicken, with potatoes and gravy. Afterward, Reb, Dodge and Jared retired to the hotel for the evening. With everyone gone, the house was unusually quiescent. Nash sought to put the girl's mind at ease as they were cleaning the last of the dishes.

'You can take the room at the boarding house, the one where Wendy was staying,' Nash offered. 'I know you must feel awkward with only the two of us here.'

'It was very nice of you to enclose the porch and put a bed there for me,' Trina said. 'I . . . I just wouldn't want people thinking poorly of you.'

He grinned. 'No one seemed to think anything of it while my sister was staying in town.'

'Yes, it is oddly quiet without Wendy.'

The remark caused Nash to laugh. 'Want to know how Wendy got her name?'

'It is quite out of the ordinary. In fact, I don't believe I ever heard of anyone with that name before.'

'Well,' Nash confided, 'her given name is Winifred Rocker Valeron. The middle name was for one of the aunts' family names. As it turned out, my sister disliked Winifred and hated the idea of being called Whinny or Rocky – Whinny resembling a horse sounding off and Rocky being a man's title. So Reese and Brett started calling her Windy – because she could talk and talk and never run out of wind. She adopted the idea and spelled it with an E to make it look better on paper. Hence, she became Wendy Valeron.'

'How appropriately charming,' Trina said, displaying a pleasant smile.

Nash paused at her pleasing expression, momentarily mesmerized by her intrinsic beauty. She noticed the fixed look and pinched her eyebrows together.

'What is it?' she asked.

Nash swallowed hard, gulping down a fleeting fantasy with more than a little effort. 'Uh, I was just. . .'

Abruptly, there came a pounding on the front door. He was saved from embarrassment, dropping the drying cloth for the dishes and hurrying through the house to open the door.

A young couple were silhouetted against the evening dusk. The girl's protruding tummy gave evidence that she was heavy with child. Her husband's face was pale with grave apprehension.

'We need a doctor! Quick!' he exclaimed. 'My wife is having pains, real bad pains!'

Nash escorted her into the examination room. She could barely waddle and her teeth were clenched as tightly closed as a tripped bear trap. Her mate followed along behind, talking rapidly.

'The pains started coming real hard about thirty minutes ago,' he informed Nash. 'The midwife who delivers most of the babies around town. . . .' He paused, then blurted, 'A couple of mothers in her care have died shortly after delivery. I . . . well, hell!' He lamented, 'I don't trust her to bring my baby into the world. And I for sure can't stand the idea of losing my Sherry.'

Trina was already putting a kettle of water on the stove to heat. She quickly gathered up some towels and joined them in the treatment room.

'I'll tend to her, my friend,' Nash told the nervous husband in a soothing tone of voice. 'If you would be so good as to wait in the outer room. We must keep the delivery area as sterile as possible.'

Trina showed him to the couch and told him not to worry. Then she returned and closed the exam room door for privacy.

Nash didn't have a lot of time. By the time he had washed up and got the girl settled on the table, the baby was on his way. It took but a few minutes before the couple had a new son.

As soon as Nash had tended to the umbilical cord, he gave the baby to Trina. She cleaned the child and had him ready for the mother's arms, by the time Nash had finished with the necessary cleansing and checking for bleeding. The delivery procedure was complete.

Moving the young mother to the patient's bed was a bit of chore, but she was stout of heart and made the few steps with only a little aid from Nash and Trina. Then, with the baby snuggled in her arms, Trina allowed the father to enter and join his family.

An hour or so later, the husband was ready to leave. He explained that they had animals on the farm so he couldn't leave them unattended.

'For the sake of precaution, we'll keep your wife and child here for a couple of days,' Nash told him. 'The biggest danger after birth is puerperal fever, also know as child-bed fever, or postpartum sepsis. Basically, it's an infection that can cause severe illness or death after childbirth.'

'I understand,' he replied. 'It's like I was saying about the midwife. The last woman she delivered for was fine for the first day or so, then she got sick and died a couple days later. It wasn't the first time it's happened, either.'

'I'm afraid it's quite common,' Nash said gravely. 'Worst of all, recent research has shown the cause is linked to midwives or doctors who fail to take proper sanitary precautions.'

'My wife was against coming here,' he admitted. 'I mean, you being a man and all. But after hearing how you saved that little girl's life. . . .' He didn't finish, but stuck out his hand. Nash accepted it in a firm shake.

'Let me know the bill,' the new father said. 'I'll sure enough make it right. Might take me till I sell some produce next month, but you can count on getting every cent.'

'Let's just get past the first couple days,' Nash said. 'Once she is home and in sound health, we can discuss payment.'

'You bet! Thanks again, Doc!'

Nash smiled at the young man's back. As the door closed, he sensed someone at his shoulder and looked over at Trina. She had a very peculiar expression on her face – maternal, yet full of wonder, and something else . . . admiration?

'How filled with gratification you must be,' she said softly. 'Mother and baby both sleeping comfortably, a new father shaking your hand, and knowing you saved the life of a young girl last week.'

'It's why I wanted to be a doctor,' he admitted. 'It isn't so fulfilling when someone walks through the door with a deadly cancer or wound or injury that is untreatable. There are numerous downsides to being in medicine too.'

'Yes, but you are trying to do good, making a sacrifice to bring relief to those who are suffering. It is a noble profession.'

'Not so noble when you see people practicing medicine who don't know squat about it, who make things worse rather than better. I'll have a talk to this midwife and point out the need for washing thoroughly. There are a lot of women who refuse to have a male doctor deliver their child due to modesty.'

'Wendy told me about your large family and their holdings, including an entire town.' Trina's brows lifted in puzzlement. 'Why didn't you go there to start your career?'

'We already have a retired Army surgeon who has been doing the doctoring for a good many years. I wouldn't have felt right to take away most or all of his business. After all, the town of Valeron only has a couple hundred people. Even with the ranch, mill, mines and such, there isn't enough to keep more than one doctor busy.'

'You could have chosen a bigger city, one with a hospital where you would be able to work a normal schedule.'

'My cousin, Wyatt, he worked a job up this way a couple years back. He told me of a young boy who was thrown from a horse. Due to there not being a doctor, the lad died. Wyatt said there were others too, stories of travelers – like the girl with the bad appendix – who came through needing help. If the people didn't find a surgeon in one of the forts along the way, many of those souls were lost.'

'You came here because the need was great,' Trina concluded.

'It's why I wanted to become a doctor,' Nash said. He

rotated his body enough that he was squared off with Trina. Her features had muted and she had a dreamy sort of look on her face, soft, inviting. . . .

The fussing of the newborn boy interrupted the moment. Trina immediately stepped back and falteringly cleared her throat. 'I'd better look in on our patients and see if they need anything.'

Nash remained standing there, his heart exposed and vulnerable, as Trina hurried off to the adjacent room.

Martin and Wendy found the laboratory office where Delacruz worked. It was a one-man research facility, upstairs, positioned over a barbershop. They knocked several times and then Martin pushed the unlocked door open. As they entered, the smell of many stringent compounds permeated the air.

After closing the door, Martin called out. 'Professor Delacruz?'

Abruptly, a man raised his head from behind a long counter of bottles, flasks, test tubes and stacks of books. His hair was mussed, shaggy, and, from the looks of it, he hadn't shaved in a few days. 'Oh!' he droned uncertainly, blinking his dark-circled, red-rimmed eyes repeatedly. 'I thought someone was at the door.'

'Yes, we knocked but. . . .'

'Tell whoever it is that I'm busy,' he said, waving a dismissive hand.

Martin opened his mouth, staring blankly at the closed door. After a moment, he said, 'Um, we are the ones who've come to see you.'

'Wonderful!' he said excitedly, his dreary greeting

completely reversed. 'You are just in time! Come over here and I'll show you.'

Martin and Wendy went around the counter and discovered a desk littered with papers and a very worn chair. The floor had debris on it from several days or weeks, bits of paper, an empty flask here or there, with used matches, a couple burned-down candles and even some string and empty cans and bottles.

'I'm Martin Valeron,' Martin made the introductions. 'This is my cousin, Wendy Valeron. My brother, Nash, sent us here to see if you could be of some help.'

'Valeron?' His brow furrowed in thought. 'I believe I knew a Valeron one time.'

'Yes, my brother said he spent some time with you to learn about different drugs or poisons.'

'Of course!' Dizzy said, showing a glimmer of understanding. 'I should have guessed.' Then he grabbed a bottle with a scribbled on label. 'This is different from black locust. I thought so! I must write that down . . . even a mild form of white snakeroot can cause distorted mental imagery.'

'It can cause what?' Wendy asked.

Dizzy scrutinized the pair, then stretched out a hand and touched Martin's shoulder. 'Um,' he said, displaying obvious confusion. 'A completely solid vision. That can't be right.'

'We came to seek your help,' Martin repeated. 'We are not a vision, we are real.'

'Of course you're real,' Dizzy sniffed diffidently. 'I mean, how else could I touch you?'

Wendy picked up a nearby piece of paper. 'This says

you are testing snakeroot.'

Dizzy snatched the piece of paper from her. 'Madam, don't be tampering with my test results. I must keep a precise record of every sensation or symptom for my research.'

Wendy sighed and looked at Martin. 'It says the effects are expected to wear off in approximately four hours.'

'When did he take it?'

'According to his notes, it has another hour or so before the time is up.'

Dizzy studied the paper, then looked back at them. He paused to examine his trembling hand. 'Ah, yes, just as I thought. Next will come prostration or queasiness. It's the anticipated. . . .' He stopped talking and closed his mouth tightly. His cheeks puffed from bile and he grabbed a nearby pail. No sooner had he emptied the contents of his stomach than he slumped to the floor.

Martin and Wendy helped him over to a cushioned Ottoman and he stretched out with his eyes closed. Rolling his head back and forth, he muttered, 'M-must write that down. Very strong reaction to such a small portion. No wonder milk sickness was so deadly to colonial settlers.'

'Would you like me to make that notation?' Wendy asked the clearly confused researcher.

His eyes popped open and he stared at her a moment. 'Why are you so . . . so blurry, young lady? I can hardly make you out.'

'I believe your vision is distorted due to the snakeroot you are testing.'

'Nonsense. You shouldn't have a symptom like . . .' He remained groggy and practically incoherent. 'What did you say you took?' he asked.

'I didn't take anything,' she answered him placidly. 'Your notes say you took a small portion of snakeroot. I'm afraid. . . .' But the man had dropped off and immediately began to snore.

'Guess we will have to wait out his experiment,' Wendy said.

Martin smiled at the situation. 'I've been accused of being too dedicated to my work, but this guy puts me to shame.'

'Yes,' Wendy agreed. 'From the looks of this place, he spends most of his time working and none of it cleaning. I bet the dust is on the shelves from the first day he moved in.'

Martin scrounged through some of the more organized stacks of papers. 'I see a dozen pages here on testing different plants and poisons. It's a wonder this guy is still alive.'

'Nash did say he was a bit odd, but he is supposed to be the best in his field.'

'Jean would string me up by my ears if my line of work was this risky.'

Wendy laughed. 'Your wife would do worse than that – she'd have you back punching cows.'

Martin sighed. 'This is the first time I've been away from her and the kids in several years. I'm not ashamed to admit I miss them terribly.'

'The hearing is in a couple days,' Wendy said. 'Soon as we prove Trina has been falsely imprisoned to steal her inheritance, you and me are going home.'

'Then you're not going to stick it out at Castle Point and become a nurse for Nash?'

'I thought I could do it, but the revulsion I feel when I see blood – it's the same as it has been all my life. I can't get past it.'

'I'm sure Nash will understand.'

Wendy flashed an impish sort of simper. 'I think he is working on someone who would make him a very fine nurse . . . and maybe a whole lot more.'

'Not Nash!' Martin snickered at the idea. 'He's a solitary bachelor. I don't remember him ever being interested in a girl. All he thought about growing up was becoming a doctor.'

'Maybe so, but you haven't been around him much lately. I can tell you, he's totally enamored when he's in the same room with Trina.' Wendy tittered like a young girl. 'If he isn't wooing her before she leaves for the trial, he'll be coming to visit her afterward.'

'And you are leaving him without a nurse,' Martin mused. 'That leaves him with a vacancy he needs to fill.'

'Yes, and Trina was very helpful during the operation he had to perform. She was impressed with his doctoring skill too, which should work in his favor.'

Before they could continue, Dizzy sat up and looked at them. 'Hello? Did I fall asleep?'

'We came to speak to you,' Wendy said. 'My brother is Nash Valeron. Do you remember him?'

'Valeron . . . I seem to know the name.'

'Yes, he said you tutored him for a time, back when he was doing his apprenticeship at the Denver hospital.'

A glimmer of recognition sparked within his eyes. 'Of course. How is Jimmy boy?'

'His name is Nash, Nash Valeron.'

'Whose name is that?'

'My brother's,' Wendy said. 'He sent us here to see you.'

'Don't be ridiculous. Jimmy wouldn't send a perfect stranger to see me.'

Wendy turned to Martin. 'I now understand why Nash thinks Mr. Delacruz can help us. If this is anything like the symptoms Trina had, it's no wonder they locked her away.'

Jared and the two long-time hands from the Valeron ranch were having supper at a café when a familiar fellow entered the room He spotted them and came over to join them.

'Wyatt!' Jared greeted him. 'I'm glad you could make it.'

'Anything for your brother. How is Nash?'

'He's got himself a damsel straight out of the game of *Rescue* we used to play,' Jared answered.

'I remember the game, although you only invited me to play when Reese was busy working.'

Jared grinned. 'I was always glad Reese was the eldest in the family. He was Pa's go-to guy, working him way more than the rest of us.'

'In our family, it was Martin who got stuck with the chores.'

'Sit down and order a meal. We will fill you in.'

The four men discussed their options throughout the meal. Before they had come up with a solid plan, Nash entered the café and walked over to them.

'I saw you ride into town a little bit ago, Wyatt,' he said, sticking out his hand. 'It's been a while.'

'What say, cuz? I hear tell you're saving lives right and left.'

Nash pulled over a chair and joined them at the table. A sheepish grin was on his face when he looked around at the others. 'Dodge . . . Reb,' he addressed the two men, 'you two never seem to age. You still look the same as when I was in my teens.'

'And you still look damp behind the ears,' Dodge teased. 'I'm surprised anyone would put their life in your hands.'

Reb also took part in the ribbing. 'Reckon when the blood is gushing, you'll trust your life to a Cheyenne medicine man, if he's the only one around.'

'You two keep up the ribbing,' Nash warned, 'and the next time you need stitching-up or break a bone, we'll round up one of those medicine men to treat you.'

That brought a round of laughter.

Wyatt took over the conversation. 'Jared was telling me you've got a fine looking gal acting as your nurse. What happened to Wendy?'

'She was forced to quit; still can't stand the sight of blood,' Nash replied. 'I've come across a few people who suffer the same reaction. It's inherent, a revulsion most people like that suffer all their lives, kind of like an allergy to certain weeds or a type of food.'

'She shouldn't waste her life in a little berg like this anyway,' Wyatt observed. 'Wendy has always been looking for big-city excitement.'

'So what's the plan . . . or do you have one yet?' Nash asked.

'We were about to put it together,' Jared explained. 'You afraid we can't watch over your little dove?'

'I thought you ought to know that I'm going with you. I'll be driving Miss Barrett in the rented carriage.'

'What?' Wyatt immediately howled his disapproval. 'You can't do that!'

'No way!' Jared sided with him. 'We can't risk you getting shot. Pa would skin us alive if something happened to his favorite son!'

But Nash held up his hand to stop any further discussion. 'Actually, that's why I came to join your little war council. I happened to be looking in the dress shop window and had an idea.'

'Let me guess,' Jared gibed. 'You think if you both wear wedding dresses, the killers won't recognize you.'

Nash grinned. 'No, I don't trust you band of yahoos to keep either of us from getting shot – no matter how we dress. And I intend to see that Trina is not harmed in any way.'

'How are you going to do that?' Jared wanted to know.

'As I said, I'll be traveling with her,' Nash said. 'If anything goes wrong in Denver, I want to be there to sort things out. I won't stand by and let Trina get sentenced to that phoney asylum again.'

Jared elbowed Wyatt, who was sitting next to him. 'See what I told you. He's smitten.'

'Begorra!' Reb shook his head in disbelief. 'You're right, Jared. The man's done lost his heart to this wayward firefly.'

CHAPTER FIVE

Lobo entered the deserted ranch house the gang had been using for a hideout. Breed had been drinking a warm beer from their limited stock. He turned in his chair and waved to Kidd.

'Lobo's back!' he called to him. 'Grab a brew for our number one scout.'

Not given to smiling, Lobo grunted his appreciation for Breed's comment and caught the bottle of beer when Kidd tossed it his way. He paused to open it, took a long pull that drained about a third of the container, then moved over and sat down on the discarded sofa – one of the four pieces of furniture the owners had left behind.

'You find out the train schedule?' Breed asked right off.

'Mama's Boy was right about that much,' he replied. 'They will have to leave on Tuesday to make the connection in Cheyenne for Denver. It will put them there the day before the hearing. If they took a later train they wouldn't make it in time.'

'Them thinking the stagecoach was too risky will be their biggest mistake, my friend.'

'I remember the route – goes through some rough

country, including a narrow pass through some foothills. It ought to be perfect for an ambush.'

'Get plenty of rest tonight and we'll start out tomorrow. We want to reach that pass well ahead of them, so we can form a nice reception. Once the job is done, we'll leave the usual Indian sign and disappear over the mesa.'

'You think Robby will come through with the rest of the money?'

'He knows better than to cross us,' Breed answered confidently. 'After all, we're handing him and his ma the deed to a fair-sized ranch. It means a lot more money to them than the small sum he is going to pay us.'

Lobo remained uneasy. 'I don't know about killing a Valeron. If I remember right, one of them is a U.S. Marshal . . . or he used to be. And there is Wyatt Valeron to consider too. That man is walking death with a gun in his hand.'

'We don't know if this character is even related to that family.'

'I'm just saying,' Lobo replied. 'We might want to keep a watch on our back-trail for a spell.'

Breed snorted. 'We won't leave any witnesses, and all of the evidence will point to a band of renegade Indians. No way anyone will link us to the killings.'

'I know you've got a head for such things,' Lobo relented. 'Besides which, one thousand dollars is one sweet payday.'

'You and me might just turn the gang over to Kidd or Mont to run for a coupla months. We could take a trip to Kansas City or Saint Louis and kick up our heels.

Either place has gambling and dance-hall gals aplenty.'

'Sounds like fun,' Lobo agreed. 'Been a long time since we just cut loose without a care.'

'It's something we will definitely do, soon as we get paid.'

Lobo held up his near-empty bottle of beer. 'I'll drink to that, Breed. I sure will.'

After an evening meal and a good night's sleep, Dizzy was more alert and suffering only minor ill effects from his lab test. Eating breakfast also seemed to clear his head. Wendy mentioned as much and Dizzy nodded.

'I get to working on something and I forget to eat.' Dizzy sighed. 'There just doesn't seem to be enough hours in the day.'

'Especially when you lose days at a time when your brain is taking a trip into a bottomless pit,' Wendy scolded him.

'Well put, young lady,' Dizzy responded.

Martin and Wendy remained at the table long after they had finished eating. Dizzy drank three cups of coffee, while the man explained about his sampling and testing different herbs, spices and poisonous plants. When he paused to take a sip, Wendy turned him toward their immediate problem.

'Nash told us you could help us determine what the phoney doctor is using to keep his patients under his control.'

Dizzy formed a blank look for a moment. 'Nash,' he repeated the name.

'Nash Valeron,' Martin clarified, 'a medical doctor

you tutored some time back, while he was doing his apprenticeship at the Denver hospital.'

'Of course,' Dizzy replied. 'Always reminded me of Jimmy boy, a childhood friend of mine.'

'Anyway, Nash thought the plant might be something like Lily of the Valley or Jimsonweed,' Martin surmised.

'And this self-professed doctor, he is controlling several patients with herbs or drugs?' Dizzy queried.

'Yes. The lady gave us a list of the symptoms she had,' Martin said, passing him a piece of paper.

Dizzy looked it over and skewed his expression. 'It could be several plants or a combination of plants. I suspect your good doctor is something of a chemist, with a background in pharmaceuticals. Otherwise, he could easily kill his subjects.'

'If we get samples from his medicine cabinet, do you think you could identify them?' Wendy asked eagerly. 'If we could prove—'

Dizzy held up a hand to stop her. 'Without the man confessing his crimes, the mere identification of these compounds or substances wouldn't be proof of anything.' He skewed his face again, resignedly. 'Plus, it might take weeks for me to isolate the different properties and make a formal determination about each drug.'

'Nash was certain you could help,' Wendy issued a plea. 'Isn't there something you can do?'

Dizzy groaned and rubbed his stomach. 'By the heavens,' he muttered under his breath. 'I may have to cut down on the number of tests I'm doing each month. I think my system is rebelling against some of these virulent plants.'

'You're lucky to still be alive, testing that stuff on yourself,' Martin told him. 'Many of those plants and flora in your research are deadly poisons.'

'I have been losing my train of thought more often lately,' Dizzy admitted. 'Just yesterday, I had a couple people show up during an experiment and I could swear I'd never seen them before.'

'If you're talking about us' – Martin said – 'you *hadn't* seen us before.'

He frowned and spoke in befuddlement. 'See what I mean?'

'About our problem,' Wendy attempted to get him back on point. 'How do we determine what kind of drugs or potions are being used on those poor patients?'

'You said something about an impending hearing . . . pertaining to the competency of this patient you are concerned about?'

'It's in three days.'

The research pharmacist threw up his hands in defeat. 'There you are!' His voice had a note of finality. 'We don't have time to . . .' Then he unexpectedly stopped the sentence, eyes fixed in a stare, as if he had suddenly been struck dumb.

After several seconds, Wendy gently prodded him. 'Mr Delacruz? Are you all right?'

A moment or two more passed, then he suddenly blinked, looked right at her and declared, 'A hearing!'

'Yes, in three days,' she told him for the second time.

Dizzy began to bob his head, a glimmer of inspiration shinning in his eyes. 'There might be a way – unortho-

dox and unethical, but it's a possibility.' He pinned
Wendy with a steady peruse. 'But only if you are willing.'
Glancing at Martin, 'If both of you are willing to go
along with a rather devious – though I might modestly
add – brilliant plan.'

'You have an idea to help Miss Barrett?' Martin asked.

'I believe it's the best way to sway a judge's ruling.
With a little luck, we might even get the doctor arrested
for his crimes in the process.'

'Wonderful!' Wendy could not contain her excitement. 'We'll do whatever is necessary!'

'First of all, I have only one question,' Dizzy said.
They both waited and he put on a curious expression.
'Who the dickens are you people, and who did you say
sent you here to see me?'

Breed and his gang reached the spot Loco had predicted would make for a good ambush. Brush- and
tree-covered hills to either side of the main trail, with a
rutted trail from where water collected after a hard rain-
storm. It meant the wagon or carriage would slow down
on the rough road, and Miss Barrett and her escort
would be sitting there – exposed like targets for shooting practice.

Breed took care with the placing of his men. Kidd
and the two Indians took up positions on the left, about
halfway up the hill, with a clear field of fire. Next, Mont
and the Pratt brothers took up similar positions on the
right, giving all six men a clean shot from less than 200
feet. Once satisfied the men were placed for the utmost
advantage, he and Lobo rode a short way down the

road. They took cover behind some bushes, remaining on horseback, ready to cut off the escape of anyone who survived the gunfire of the deadly ambush.

'You're sure it's the right people coming?' he asked Lobo.

'Just the two of them, riding in an open buggy with a cloth canopy. The gal is decked out in a blue dress and that Valeron joker is wearing a brown suit and hat. I didn't see anyone else, just the two of them.'

'They must feel confident about making the journey alone,' Breed said. 'I've got to wonder why they didn't hire a couple of gunmen to tag along?'

'If her escort is a Valeron, he's probably too arrogant to think he needs any help.'

'Man's got to be a fool. Having an important name won't protect you. . . .' Breed chuckled. 'Not from a bunch of ignorant savages who don't listen to gossip or read newspapers.'

Lobo also laughed. 'Yeah, what does a raiding party of renegade Indians know about reputations?'

The two of them stood in their stirrups, peeking through the foliage, able to see the buggy as it came around the bend. The horse had a steady gait, while the two passengers were totally unaware that death was waiting a short distance away. They approached steadily, slowing for the ruts, and continuing directly to the planned killing field. The serenity of the morning was disturbed only by the sounds of a chirping bird and the single horse pulling the open buggy with only a cloth canopy. Breed and Lobo could see the two travelers now, sitting side by side, rigid and untroubled, without a care—

Booming gunfire from six rifles opened up simultaneously, shattering the stillness.

The two occupants of the buggy were riddled with several bullets each, folding downward under the deadly barrage, collapsing at once from the direful assault. Confused, the horse simply stopped, dancing in place, spooked by the shooting, but uncertain of which direction to go.

Breed and Lobo broke cover and started forward to inspect their kill. Suddenly, a second set of rifles commenced to fire from somewhere higher up in the hills.

'It's a trap!' Lobo shouted.

Breed pulled back on the reins, scanning the slope of the hillside in time to see Mont and the Pratt boys were all down. The opposite side was taking fire too. Kidd managed to get to his horse, but Claw and Hawk were both knocked off their feet. As Kidd fled the scene at a gallop, Lobo grunted at his side.

'I'm hit!' he yelped.

'Come on!' Breed cried, swinging his horse about. 'Let's get out of here!'

They dug in their heels, driving their horses away from the scene as fast as the animals could carry them, riding low over the saddle to reduce the chance of getting hit by anyone still shooting at them. Somehow, the ambush had turned into a deadly trap – not only for the two people in the buggy – but for him and his gang!

Reb was crawling out of the half door, under the seat of the carriage, as Jared arrived. He quickly looked him over.

'You OK?'

'The iron plates we put under the seat cushions sure enough protected me,' Reb replied, 'but with all that heat, I earned a real sympathy for a pot roast. I been sweating buckets in that little crawl space, especially while having to drive the rig.'

'You did great!' Jared praised his efforts. 'Looks like Nash's idea worked perfectly.'

'Just like we planned,' Reb agreed. 'Soon as the shooting started, I loosened the rope holding the two dummies and let them topple over.'

'Real inspirational putting clothes on those dress forms from the lady's clothing store. The straw stuffing sure enough worked.'

'Yeah, doggie,' Reb agreed. 'Them bullets sounded like cannons when they were hitting the seat cushion. Tell you what, I would have liked to have been protected with one of them there steel plates when the Yankees were shooting at me up at Missionary Ridge.'

Wyatt arrived on his horse to join them. A satisfied grin was on his face. 'Got two of them on our side,' he informed Jared. 'I see you didn't miss a one.'

'I always was better than you with a rifle,' Jared teased. 'The first two went down before the third man knew they were being shot at. He almost made it to his horse before I got him in my sights.'

'Took us longer to get in position,' Wyatt said. 'We weren't quite ready when you opened fire, so we were a little slow joining the foray. One got away, but we figured the two Indians were the more capable. I told Dodge to make sure we got them first. If they had gotten into the brush, we might have been here all day trying to root them from cover.'

'Good call on where the attack would be,' Reb commended Jared. 'You spoiled what would have been an easy double killing for that gang.'

'Reb hit it squarely on the head, cuz,' Wyatt added his praise. 'I still don't know how you managed to discover the men lying in ambush without giving yourself away.'

'I think I grazed one of the two on horseback,' Jared returned to the gang. 'They were a long way off and their horses were dancing around some.'

'Either that, or you're getting rusty,' Wyatt joked.

Dodge came down to join them about the time a second buggy appeared on the trail. This time it wasn't a pair of dummies, being driven by an unseen driver in the space beneath the seat cushion.

'Here they are, safe and sound,' Wyatt announced, upon their arrival.

The girl had a worried look on her face, but there was nothing to see but the two dress forms lying on the seat of the other buggy.

'Everyone all right?' Nash asked.

'You are both going to need a new set of clothes,' Jared remarked. 'The dress and suit each got a few holes in them.'

'Better the clothes than our hides,' Nash retorted. 'How many got away?'

'Three,' Wyatt answered. 'They weren't taking any chances; they attacked with eight men.'

'Eight men!' Trina gasped. 'You mean . . . you had to kill. . . '

'We pretty much eliminated a pack of cutthroat killers,' Jared informed her. 'These fellows put a half dozen holes in what they thought were you and Nash. Had we taken them alive, we'd have hanged them on the spot.'

'Jared's right,' Nash said, looking at her. 'There's no law this side of Cheyenne. Murdering bandits can't be allowed a chance to ever kill again. Justice on the frontier has to be swift to prevent everyone from living in constant fear.'

'Soon as we gather up the bodies, I'll pick up the trail of the three who got away,' Jared advised his brother and Wyatt.

'I'll report this attack to the authorities and see about wanted posters or rewards,' Wyatt said. 'Reb and Dodge, you two help load the dead on the outlaws' horses or the spare buggy. We'll stick with Nash the rest of the way to Cheyenne . . . just in case those three try again.'

'Dodge can drive the carriage – we'll tether the animals in a string behind him – and I'll scout ahead for us,' Reb outlined. 'We won't give them a second chance to ambush us.'

Wyatt turned to Jared. 'You go ahead and get on their trail. Just be careful. There are still three of them to deal with.'

'I'm sure they had a plan to hide their tracks,' he replied. 'It might take me some time, but I'll run them to ground.'

'Soon as things are squared away in Cheyenne, I'll try and figure a way to join you. Send a wire if you pass a trading post or some place where you can send word to Cheyenne. If I don't hear from you in a day or two, I'll start out on my own.'

'Remember the doctor's hired men and that Robby character,' Jared warned. 'Nash might need your help.'

'We'll tend to them, cuz. Just don't get in over your head with those three. If you need—'

'Sure,' Jared interrupted with a smirk, 'I won't be too proud to ask.' Then with a tad more sincerity, 'I sent for you to help with this, didn't I?'

Wyatt raised a hand in farewell. 'See you.'

Turk entered Callisto's office with a telegram in hand. The doctor raised his head from his paperwork expectantly. 'Well?'

'It ain't from the Gowans telling us good news. It looks more like someone wanting to be rid of a troublesome relative or such.'

Callisto took the paper and quickly read it. 'Yes, I believe you're right. It says this person heard about Restful Acres and wants to set up a meeting. 'He studied it for a moment. 'They would like to get together the night before the trial.'

'Could that be one of them there coincidences?'

'Probably. This has no bearing on the case, just a consultation about an abusive husband.'

Turk uttered a grunt of conceit. 'Word is getting around, boss. We might have to add on a couple more rooms if you keep taking on new patients.'

The doctor laughed. 'Besides which, I might have to hire another person or two to help you and Manny. Be kind of nice to have an extra attendant to share the work load.'

78

'No argument here, so long as it don't mean a cut in pay.'

'More patients means more money.'

'Except for the simple-minded twins,' Turk complained.

'Yes, the State only pays a small fee each month for keeping them – hardly worth our time. However, we need them to cement our position as an asylum for troubled minds. If we took only wealthy individuals, suspicion might be raised that we were not legitimate.'

'I like the way you use the legal term – *legitimate*,' Turk praised the doctor's terminology. 'It's no wonder ain't nobody ever questioned your credentials.'

Callisto looked over the telegram message a second time. 'Have Manny ride over to the trading post and send a reply. I will meet with this woman and see what she has to say.'

'And make certain she can afford our services!' Turk added with a grin.

The lawman walked around the five bodies, having laid them out next to the carpenter's shop – he being the one who built coffins for burial. A deputy had already compared the men to wanted circulars and come up with a match on three of them.

'These men are from a known renegade band,' Jake Bender remarked. 'They've been raising hell since I was appointed to office. Not so much here in Cheyenne, but all over the country.'

'It would seem the leader is one of those who got away,' Wyatt said. 'My cousin is tracking them, so we should get them all.'

Jake's brows lifted in an arch. 'Your brother that good, is he?'

Wyatt grinned. 'Jared could follow an ant through a forest if he put his mind to it. He's got a knack for reading sign and has always been half-bloodhound.'

'The rewards for three of these men is $100 each, but no one ever knew who the Indians were or from which tribe.'

'We didn't shoot them for the bounty,' Wyatt told him. 'We shot them for ambushing and trying to kill an innocent woman and her escort.'

'And this has to do with who takes ownership of the Barrett ranch outside of Denver?' he asked, having listened to Wyatt's original explanation of the events.

'That's right. We've got more fish to fry, so I'd like to get this cleared up as soon as possible.'

'What about the reward? It will take a few days to get payment.'

'Send it to my cousin's place: Nash Valeron, up at Castle Point. He's a doctor, just started his practice. He can use the funds to add on a room or two for handling more patients.'

'Sounds like a good investment,' Jake said. 'And if your other cousin can bring in the missing three from the gang, he can collect another $500. That there Breed is worth $300, being that he is the known leader of the band.'

'We'll get him.'

'If you need some help, I can get you a deputy to ride along.'

'Thanks, Jake,' Wyatt said, 'but me and Jared can handle the chore. Besides, I know you have your hands full with all of the trail herds, soldiers and freighters here in Cheyenne.'

'I could use another dozen men – that's a fact.' He grinned. 'Of course, if I had a man like you, I could forget the other eleven deputies.'

Wyatt laughed. 'I believe you overestimate my prowess as a lawman, Jake.'

'I heard the tale about Brimstone,' Jake told him, growing serious. 'You took the Waco Kid in a standup, straight out gunfight!' He clicked his tongue. 'I'd have given a month's salary to have been there to see that.'

'Waco had been living the high life, using his reputation to walk tall among the common outlaws, rustlers and petty gunmen, instead of staying sharp by practising his craft. For men who live by the gun, that's a fatal mistake.'

'Guess you proved your point.'

'I wouldn't have wanted to go up against him in his prime, Jake.'

'Well,' the lawman returned to the business at hand, 'if you need some help, you only have to send word. This country will be a whole lot safer when men like Breed and Lobo are no longer robbing and killing.'

Wyatt shook the man's hand and left to join up with Reb and Dodge. The two ranch hands were busy dealing the two buggies and horses to the local livery. It would mean taking a loss, but they had come out ahead with the reward money.

As it happened, Wyatt met the two men coming up

the street. They arrived to meet him a few steps away from the jail.

'Done pretty good,' Reb spoke first, holding out a wad of bills. 'Man said he would have given us more, but the one carriage has a number of bullet holes in it.' He chuckled. 'Did allow us fifty cents each for the two steel plates.'

Dodge joined in, 'We stabled the horses for the night, so we're as free as birds. And I reckon there's enough money for us to get a room and have a decent meal tonight.'

Wyatt accepted the money and tucked it away. 'We need to make arrangements at the train station to have our horses loaded in the stock car tomorrow. Then we'll tend to eating and finding a room.'

'Glad those dead bodies are done with and behind us,' Dodge said. 'Always have a nervous feeling when doing something like that. I'm afeared that one day a sheriff or marshal will decide to toss our sorry bones in a cell for killing someone they knew. I mean, it ain't as if every lawman is honest or trustworthy.'

'Jake seems to be both of those things,' Wyatt replied. 'He offered information about the rewards without my having to ask. A crooked lawman might have *forgot* to mention there was a bounty, then collected it himself.'

'Wyatt's right,' Reb assured his pal. 'Let's hope the Denver police are as honest and trustworthy as Jake. After all, we're going after one of their well-thought-of citizens, a man who calls himself a doctor.'

'I'll wager Martin and Wendy have devised a plan by this time.' Wyatt chuckled. 'Martin sure came up with a winner of an idea for the ambush. You riding under the seat, protected by steel plates – and the dummies?'

'Didn't know he had it in him.' Reb also laughed. ' 'Course, that mightn't have worked a'tall, if Jared hadn't been scouting ahead and found where them fellers were waiting.'

'Never met an Indian any better at stealth,' Wyatt extolled Jared's abilities.

'Well, I hope Martin comes up with a second plan that's equal to this last one.'

'And if not?' Dodge asked. 'A blind man could see the way Nash looks at that charming little flower. Ain't no way he's gonna stand by and let them toss her in a lunatic asylum again.'

'Same goes for me too,' Reb vowed. 'Miss Barrett seems as right as rain. I won't be shy about sticking my nose in, if'n they try and imprison her again.'

'Let's get squared away about our horses,' Wyatt told them. 'Then we'll get something to eat and turn in. The train departs fairly early in the morning, so we won't be drinking at a saloon tonight or sleeping late.'

'We're with you, Wyatt,' Dodge spoke for the pair of riders. 'Just like out at the ranch; one of you Valerons lead, and we follow.'

'Right through the gates of hell, if need be!' added Reb.

Wyatt chuckled. 'Boys, I'm going to talk to Martin when this is all said and done. You two deserve a raise.'

CHAPTER SIX

Kidd cleaned and bandaged the crease on the side of Lobo's hip. The bullet had carved a three inch groove through the flesh below the hip bone, but it was not too deep. It had bled a little, but wrapping a cloth around his waist to cover the injury pretty much took care of the wound.

Breed had taken the temporary stop to look over their back-trail. He arrived as Kidd was tying a knot in the bandage.

'Ain't bad,' Kidd told him. 'Still, it's going to hurt while we're riding.'

'Can't be helped,' Breed said. 'We've got a shadow. I caught sight of him; he's about a half mile behind us. Would have missed him if I hadn't used my field glasses. He was right on our tracks, moving at a pretty good pace.'

'We'll lose him at the hard-pan on the mesa,' Lobo spoke with confidence. 'Once going over the rock and shale, he'll be left behind scratching his head.'

'That's right,' Kidd said. 'How many posses have we

lost up on the mesa – a dozen?'

Breed sat atop his horse, allowing the animal to snatch a bite of tall grass. It wasn't a good habit for a horse to get into, but the animal would need its strength.

'We take no chances,' he explained to the others. 'Once we reach hard ground, we start our zigzag, then we reverse our direction. If need be, we'll set up an ambush and pay back whoever it is tracking us. We owe him for the deaths of three of our men and the Pratt brothers.'

'We could set up for him now,' Lobo suggested. 'Two of us can get off the trail, while all three horses continue. He'll walk right to us.'

'Don't forget, that very thinking got Mont and our Indian friends kilt,' Kidd tossed out the reminder. 'If we ambush him, I want a huge advantage, and I mean a very huge advantage.'

'You going yella on us?' Lobo challenged.

'If I had been one second slower getting to cover, I'd be dead now!' Kidd barked his response. 'And on the other side, the Pratt boys and Mont weren't so lucky. I could hear them being killed – by a single rifleman.' He put a hard stare on Lobo. 'You get that? One man put all three of them down ... with one shot each!' He snorted his contempt. 'I'm not fool enough to take on someone with that kind of skill, not without every advantage in the world working in my favor!'

'Enough talk,' Breed silenced the pair. 'We'll lose him on the mesa, by using the same tricks that worked on every other posse we've had to shake. If he shows up down the road in a day or two, then we will deal with him.'

'Speaking of down the road,' Lobo said. 'Where we going?'

'To pay Robby a visit. He set us up.'

'What?' Kidd cried. 'No way!'

'Why would he do that?' Lobo wanted to know. 'What would he have to gain?'

Breed waved his hand to stop the protests. 'I'm not saying he did it on purpose, but he sure enough gave away our plan. Who else knew when and where we were going to go after that girl?' He paused to spit. 'No one! That's who!'

'So,' Kidd postulated, 'you figure he ran his mouth and Valeron learned of a possible attack.'

'We were all taken in by the wagon and its two fake dummies – filled with straw or something. I don't know how they got the horse to pull the buggy like it did, but those two targets weren't alive.'

'And the gunmen opened up on us within a few seconds.' Kidd was now thinking along the same lines. 'How is that possible?'

'Our tracker back there,' Lobo suggested. 'He could have sniffed out our location before the wagon arrived. I'll bet he split up his force to cover both sides of the trail. Then when we started to shoot, they rushed forward to a position where they could kill us all.'

'There's no doubt,' Breed pledged, 'Robby is respon-sible . . and we're going to collect the balance of what he owes us.'

'And then?' Lobo wanted to know.

'Then we kill him!'

*

Nash and Trina took their meal alone, before retiring to the hotel in Cheyenne for the night. The girl maintained a disquieting silence, avoiding eye contact and contributing almost no conversation. Nash allowed her the tranquility without reproach, mentioning little more than an observation about the way the meal was prepared and offering to buy her something for dessert. He did not blame her for being worried – her ranch and freedom were both at stake.

On the walk back to the hotel, Trina did hook her arm though his and stayed close to his side. He kept a slow pace and paused to browse at store windows along the walk. When they reached the entrance to the hotel, Trina balked at the door.

'I . . . I need to . . .' she said haltingly. 'Mr Valeron, I. . . .'

'It's getting cool,' Nash said. 'And you don't have a wrap.'

'I'm warm enough,' she countered. 'Besides, there isn't any wind, so it's pleasant enough.'

'There's a bench in front of the dry goods store,' he suggested. 'The place is closed, so I don't think anyone will mind if we sit down for a minute.'

Trina accompanied him and they sat down together. After a short and awkward silence, the young lady finally turned to look directly at him.

'I'm sorry, Mr Valeron,' she murmured. 'I can't help it. I . . . I'm terrified of returning to Denver.'

Nash reached out and took her hand. 'I would prefer

you call me Nash,' he said gently. 'I believe we know each other well enough to do away with titles.'

She reacted to his offer with a tight smile. 'Yes, I've shared your home, gotten to know your sister and brother, and even a couple of your cousins.'

'More importantly,' he said easily, 'you've helped with a delicate operation and the delivery of a baby. That pretty much makes us co-workers.'

She laughed. 'Who would have known? Me, doing the chores of a nurse in a hospital.'

'A very competent nurse at that.'

Her eyes revealed pleasure at his compliment, but she became serious once more. 'What is going to happen to me? Do you think Martin and Wendy can get the evidence I need?'

'Dizzy is a genius,' Nash stated assuredly. 'He is a trifle odd, probably from all the testing he does on himself. But, if he can determine the compound or specific plant being used on you and the other patients, we should have a good argument in court.'

'It will be my word against a medical professional, a well-respected doctor who oversees people with mental problems.'

Nash took her second hand, holding them both tightly, physically transmitting his solemn bond or promise. 'I can only ask you to trust me,' he said. 'We are not going to let them put you back under Callisto's care – no matter what!'

'What if the judge rules—'

'No matter what!' Nash reiterated. 'If it takes another medical doctor's opinion, we will get it. If they try to take you by force, we won't allow it.'

'How can you stop them?'

'Martin knows the law. He can make a legal argument to keep you out of the doctor's hands until we get a second opinion.'

'I want to believe you, Nash,' she said, her eyes glistening with restrained tears. 'I do. It's just that I . . . I. . . .'

'Trina,' Nash whispered, 'I promise, I won't desert you.'

She lowered her head, seeking to maintain her decorum. 'I'm sorry,' she murmured. 'I can't face the idea of going back there – the degradation, the hopelessness, being treated like a caged animal – I am so afraid.'

Nash pulled her closer to him and slipped his arms around her, consoling her as he would an injured or frightened child. She rested her head on his shoulder and they remained that way for a short span of time.

'I've never had time to seek out a courtship with a woman,' Nash finally broke the silence. "I've been too busy learning everything I could about medicine and starting my own practice.' He took a deep breath and released it slowly. 'Having met you, it has changed the way I feel about medicine, about life.'

Trina sat back and looked squarely at him. 'You are a very good man, Nash Valeron.'

'It's opened my eyes. I want something more than to just help people. I would like to be something more than a rescuer or protector.'

Trina displayed a curious mien. 'Are you saying you

want to court me?'

'Yes, something like that.'

'But I have a life to reclaim, a ranch to run,' Trina said in an unusually husky voice. 'It's all that's kept me alive for these past few months.'

'And we'll get that ranch back for you,' Nash vowed.

'A hundred and fifty miles is a long way to come calling, especially when you have to be at your office to help the wounded, sick and injured.'

'It would help if I knew you were. . . ' He hesitated, searching for the right words. '. . . interested in spending time with me.'

Trina glanced up and down the street. The night lamps had been lit, but the walkway was mostly dark shadows. Rather than reply, she leaned over and very gently kissed Nash on the cheek. When she pulled back, he could tell she was blushing from being so forward, but her features were soft and inviting.

'I think,' she said softly, 'we should put any future relationship on hold, until we know if you would be coming out to my ranch or visiting me at the lunatic asylum.'

Nash had to clear his throat before he could muster forth any words. 'Yeah, OK. I can go along with that.'

Robby entered the house still swearing oaths and cussing. Lucile was seated in a rocking chair in front of the living room fireplace. She had been reading the Denver newspaper.

'I don't like it when you sound off like that,' she said, setting the paper down on a small table next to her rocker. 'Do I want to know why you are swearing like a mule skinner?'

'The attack failed!' he blurted out. 'It was some kind of trick. Five of Breed's men were killed and he's on the run.'

'What?' she gasped. 'But you said—'

'Yeah, Mother!' Robby snapped angrily. 'I know what I said. It should have been easy – over a half dozen men ambushing one or two men and a woman. I don't even know all of the details, but the telegraph message from Cheyenne said there were five bodies for the cemetery and Breed is in the wind.'

'Of all the incompetence!' Lucile was on her feet now, storming around the room. 'That means that spiteful little witch will show up in court.'

'Do you think Callisto can convince a judge she is crazy?'

The woman stopped pacing and put her hands on her hips. 'He knows the terms to use,' she said. 'It won't be the first time he's testified at a hearing.' She ground her teeth together in an attempt to suppress her rage. 'This shouldn't have been necessary! Trina ought to either be dead or back in the doctor's custody!'

Robby asked, 'What are our chances with the judge?'

'Callisto told me he has never lost at one of those hearings.' She also mouthed a profanity. 'How did this go so wrong?'

'It must have been that Valeron character,' Robby said, his expression one of wonder. 'How do you think he managed to get safely past Breed and his men? I mean, five bodies! Five!'

'What am I,' she snarled like a cornered badger, 'a witch with some special vision to see an event a hundred miles away? How should I know what went wrong?'

Robby did not hide his vexation. 'This could mean more trouble than we expected, Mother. After I hired Breed to do the job, I ran into a man who knew a little about the Valerons. Evidently, they are a large family with a reputation for upholding justice. The Valeron in Castle Point is a doctor, but his brother, the one who befriended Trina, is Jared Valeron. He hanged several men who kidnapped his sister some time back. This guy I met said Jared Valeron was the best tracker and rifle-man in the territory.'

'That doesn't explain how Trina and him got through an ambush unscathed.'

'No, but the fellow also said the Valerons all shared a strong family bond – if one Valeron had some trouble, several more would answer the call for help. I'm betting that's what happened. Jared Valeron must have wired for help to take on Breed's gang.'

Lucile wrung her hands nervously. 'How much money do we have from the last cattle sale?'

'A couple thousand, but $500 of that is owed to Breed.'

'Breed failed to do his job! We don't owe him any-thing.'

'What's your thinking, Mother?'

'We better put together some traveling bags, in case the judge rules against us.'

'You said Callisto could handle the hearing.'

'And you said Breed would eliminate Trina without a

hitch!' Lucile's lips pressed into a tight line. 'Robby,' she said tightly, 'we won't panic yet, but we better have a plan if we lose in court. Trina might sic the law on us. We need to be ready to run.'

'Run where?'

'Anywhere we can start over,' she told him. 'With a couple thousand dollars, we can buy a small business or ranch . . . a long, long way from here.'

'I'll keep a couple of the best horses in the barn and pack a bag. The money is hidden in the root cellar.'

'Let's hope we don't need to leave at all, but these Valerons might be a bigger pain than we are prepared to handle.'

'Whatever you say, Mother,' Robby said. 'I'll be ready.'

'How you feeling this morning?' Breed asked Lobo, as the man gingerly sat up in his blankets.

'I'm a little sore, but the wound looks clean. I can still ride.'

'Kidd is checking the back trail, looking for any sign of the tracker.'

'We've used this mesa for an escape a dozen times and have never been caught,' Lobo bragged. 'I don't see this guy being any better than some of the trackers on those posses.'

'All the same, we'll keep a cold camp and get by with jerky, tins of beans, and hard rolls, while in the saddle.'

'You think it's safe to turn towards Robby's ranch?'

Breed considered his answer for a moment then nodded. 'We'll stay on our westerly direction and keep a sharp eye till noon or so. If we don't catch sight of anyone behind us, we can make our turn. It's still a two day ride to Robby's spread.'

Kidd returned as Breed was helping Lobo put on his boots. He shook his shoulders and rubbed his hands together.

'Br-r-r-r, it's getting cool in the mornings,' he said. 'Wish we had some hot coffee on a nice warm fire.'

'Maybe tonight,' Breed allowed. 'Once we know no one is doggin' our trail.'

Kidd said, 'I didn't see anything moving, other than a doe and her fawn. I think we lost him.'

'Maybe he's a late riser,' Lobo joked. 'He might be over the next hill.'

'Exactly why we're going to continue going west. Soon as we're certain there's no one behind us, we can swing south and head for Robby's ranch.'

Kidd stared at Breed. 'We gonna kill him?'

'Mont, the Pratt boys and our Indian friends are dead. What would you have us do?'

'I'd get the money owed to us first,' Kidd said. 'We might have to leave this part of the country, what with the Valerons looking for us.'

'One good thing,' Lobo threw into the conversation, 'we didn't hurt any of them.'

'What are you talking about?' Kidd wanted to know.

'The Pratt boys weren't too keen on the job when I told them there was a Valeron involved. Guess they had heard some talk about that bunch.'

'You didn't say anything about it,' Breed said.

'No, it didn't seem to matter. We were going to blame

94

it on renegade Indians.'

'What'd the Pratts know about them?' Kidd enquired.

'Seems the Valeron family has a rigid code of justice, if you harm or kill one of their own. We didn't harm or kill anyone . . . unless you count the two dummies they used to fool us.'

'Then you figure they will give up,' Breed made the statement.

'Be my guess.'

Breed arched his back to relieve the stiffness from a night's sleep on the cold, hard ground. 'We won't count them out of this until we have our money. We get as far away as Kansas or the Dakotas without any sign of them, then we'll erase the Valerons from our past.'

CHAPTER SEVEN

The mesa was the perfect place to lose a posse. Jared had been forced to follow on foot, searching for any partial horseshoe imprint, a stone freshly turned, the slightest scrape if it looked recent. With a number of elk, deer and trails used by men driving cattle or even the occasional renegade Indian, every animal print was a distraction, misleading a tracker, causing him to lose sight of the actual trail he was trying to follow.

Darkness had forced him to stop and he had to wait for daylight to start again. Hour after hour he moved at a snail's pace, but it was necessary. If he lost the three riders, he might never locate their tracks again. The huge plateau covered many square miles. It would have taken days to ride a full circle in hopes of finding the trail of three horses leaving the mesa. He didn't have that kind of time. He needed to stay on their heels and determine their route. If he learned where they were going, then he could attempt to make up ground and possibly catch them.

The sun was high overhead when Jared found a slight

depression within a stand of pinon. It had been the bedding down spot for a deer or elk, but a thorough search revealed the heel print of a man. The trio had been careful, but someone had stepped near the drip-line of one of the larger trees. It was just soft enough to leave an incomplete boot print! Five minutes of search-ing and he found where three horses had been on a picket line. The freshest of the droppings were only a few hours old.

'Gotcha!' Jared said under his breath.

His heart began to pound as he remained perfectly still and scanned the area as far as he could see. Once satisfied there was no sound of horses moving, and – thankfully – no bullet came from an assailant's gun, he determined the direction they had taken.

The three men were in more of hurry now, thinking they had surely lost the man on their back-trail. It was the first mistake along their escape route, an act of con-fidence which they should not have indulged. Jared was soon atop his mount, still moving slowly, but steadily and with purpose. It wasn't far to the rim of the mesa. As soon as the fugitives were down among the rolling hill countryside, the trail would be easier to read and Jared would begin to close the gap between them.

'Thought you had it made, didn't you?' Jared said aloud. 'Well, think again, you bushwhacking varmints. I'm comin' for you . . . and there's hell to pay!'

It was the most exclusive restaurant in Denver, a suitable meeting place for a person with a lot of money to burn. Nash, in the guise of a manservant, had visited the place earlier and used a sizable tip to get the reservation and make special arrangements ahead of time.

Wendy, attired in an expensive evening gown and with her hair professionally styled earlier in the day, introduced herself at the reservation counter. A refined gentleman, in an immaculate suit, presented himself as the Maitre d' and led her to a secluded corner of the dining room. He held her chair, professionally placed a napkin over her lap, and told her the special wine her servant had provided would be served as soon as her guest arrived.

Nervous did not begin to cover how she felt, yet there was an inner excitement, a feeling of queasy apprehension mixed with a covert eagerness. This was exciting, devious, intense, all wrapped up in a blanket of exhilaration and intrigue. She had an inkling of how Brett Valeron's wife must have felt when she was working for the Pinkerton agency.

A gentleman arrived with the Maitre d' a few moments later. He was moderately good looking, had a sophistication about him, with nicely groomed hair, a perfectly fitted suit and string tie over a silk shirt. His shoes were polished bright enough to have been used as mirrors.

'Ah, Mrs Vandermeer, I presume!' he greeted her.

She bid him a welcoming smile. 'Dr Callisto?'

He bowed shortly, took the chair opposite her and continued to display a professional smile. 'I hope I didn't keep you waiting. You said seven o' clock?'

'Yes,' she replied. 'I'm one of those people who is always a bit more punctual than required. It drives my husband crazy.'

Callisto laughed dryly. 'I'm afraid his complaint of one of your quirks is not enough to have him committed to an institution.'

She rewarded his jest with a smile. They took time to order from the menu and were presented with a bottle of wine. 'As you requested,' the waiter politely informed Wendy.

'Thank you,' she reciprocated.

He poured each of them a glass of wine and left to tend to other patrons.

Callisto took a drink, nodded his approval at the wine selection, then got down to business.

'So tell me,' he queried. 'This problem with your husband. Is it something you and he cannot work out amiably?'

'Elbert is a habitual drinker, Doctor. Most often it is hard liquor,' she told him in a confiding tone of voice. 'When he drinks too much, he is also a hitter.' She paused to add significance to the term. 'I was raised a proper lady and I've grown weary of making excuses for my bruises and black eyes.'

'I don't know what you've heard about our services, Mrs Vandermeer, but there has to be proof a person is mentally unsound before we can admit him to Restful Acres.'

The meal arrived and they began to eat. For a time, the subjects were fashion, politics and everyday social events. While Wendy maintained her subterfuge by not being overeager to suggest anything underhanded or illegal, she eventually got back to her husband.

'Doctor, I must confess, I can think of no alternatives. Elbert has gotten worse over the past year and my own family has fallen on hard times. A fire destroyed the company my father built back East and most of the inventory was lost. He had to go deeply into debt to start anew. I have begged Elbert to join with him as a partner or help them financially, but my husband is as tightfisted as a miser down to his last dime. He barely provides me with enough of an allowance to keep a suitable wardrobe and purchase the needed weekly supplies for the house.'

'So you have a limited amount of money.'

Wendy did not miss the slight clouding of his expression. She leaned forward. 'If he were to be put away in your asylum, I would gain immediate access to his fortune.'

'For such a man, a man of his importance, the expense would be quite steep.' Callisto waved a dismissive hand. 'But it is foolish to talk about it, so long as Elbert does not exhibit any signs of mental difficulty.'

'I didn't contact you by random chance, Doctor,' Wendy confided. 'I had a private little chat with Mrs. Freeman. I believe you are treating her husband, Horace, who was known to frequent saloons and parlors, and even had a mistress.'

Callisto outwardly relaxed at her being acquainted with the Freemans. 'Yes, it took a little extra effort for us to convince a judge that Horace had lost his sense of reason. He had several friends who stood by him.'

'My husband has mostly enemies who would be glad to be rid of him.' She raised an inquisitive eyebrow. 'So how did you manage to win the Freeman case?'

'His wife slipped a little medicine into his coffee the morning of the hearing . . . and he attacked the judge.' He chuckled at the memory. 'Frightened the old man so bad, he summoned two courthouse attendants to physically remove Mr Freeman from the room.'

'How would I go about seeing to it that Elbert suffered a similar loss of faculties?'

'It depends on his habits. Like, for instance, does he have coffee or tea each morning or take a bit of brandy each night?'

'Yes, to both of those.'

'If you could provide me with some particulars – his approximate height and weight is needed, so we don't over medicate – then we might figure a way to get him out of your life. However, to remove any suspicion, you would have to slip the tonic into his drinks over a period of time. That way, he would progressively get worse and appear to lose his mind a little at a time. A total break all at once is rare and is usually brought on by a traumatic event like a death in the family. As I said before, it would be quite expensive to undertake a job of this kind.'

Wendy prompted a sly simper to her lips and added a slight flutter of her eyelashes. 'Dr Callisto, I assure you, to be rid of that man, I would be very generous indeed.'

'I would need a token of your generosity up front.'

Wendy pursed her lips. 'I have been holding back a little of the housekeeping money for several weeks. I can also sell an item or two from my jewelry collection if need be. Would $500 be sufficient to get started?'

'For a down payment,' he said. 'We can discuss the monthly expense next time we meet.'

'I understand.'

'We will sit down and set a timetable. You can give me a list of information about your husband – his likes, passions, personality, that sort of thing. It will help with the choice of ingredients needed to get the reaction we want.' He laughed. 'Wouldn't do to dose him with something and have him lose control and hurt you.'

Wendy also laughed. 'No, having him kill me would negate the deal and both of us would lose a great deal of money.'

Callisto grinned and finished the last of his drink. 'You're a woman after my own heart,' he said. 'Drop me a note when you wish to get together again. I need a day's notice so I can cover the work at the asylum.'

'I'll be in touch.'

Wendy discreetly placed money for the dinner next to his plate. The doctor rose to his feet, held her chair, and they exited the restaurant together.

Being a gentleman, Callisto also escorted her to the entrance of the hotel. They parted there – he going his own way and Wendy headed off to her room.

Nash, Wyatt and Trina arrived at the Delacruz apartment as Martin and Dizzy were preparing to go to the hotel and wait for Wendy's return.

'Dizzy!' Nash greeted him. 'How've you been doing?'

'Tommy boy!' Dizzy exclaimed. 'What are you doing here?'

Nash laughed. 'Not Tommy – it's Nash, Nash Valeron,

from the Denver hospital.'

The man's face lit up with recognition. 'Of course, I remember. Are you still doing your apprenticeship work?'

'No, I've opened my own office up at Castle Point.'

'And is this your sweetheart?' he wanted to know, looking at Trina. 'She is much too pretty to not have someone seeking her hand.'

Martin spoke up. 'This is the girl we are trying to prove is sane.'

Dizzy took a step closer to the girl and stared right into her eyes. She leaned away from such an intense scrutiny, but held her ground.

'Eyes are clear, no flush or tenseness. Are you suffering any hallucinations or cramping?'

'I've been free of the treatments for over two weeks,' Trina responded. 'I'm fine.'

'Of course you are, young lady. It's just as I was told. The phoney doctor had you under his control via the medication he forced you to take. What a scoundrel. Someone ought to do something about him.'

'We are doing something about him,' Martin reminded Dizzy. 'Remember?'

Dizzy started to answer back, but paused to stare at Wyatt. 'Hello? Are you a friend of Tommy boy?'

'I'm Martin's brother,' Wyatt informed him. 'Nash is my cousin.'

'Nash?' He appeared puzzled.

'He's talking about me, Dizzy,' Nash said. 'You do recall me warning you about doing too much testing on yourself?'

Dizzy laughed. 'Well, who else is going to volunteer to let me dose them with poisons?' Then he lowered his voice, speaking to Wyatt. 'You should see the tonic we've put together. I hate to praise my own cooking, but I may one day discover a drug to ease anyone's misery.'

'Where is Wendy?' Nash asked Martin.

'She met with Dr Callisto for a dining engagement. If need be, she can testify against him tomorrow.' Martin hurried to add, 'That is, if she got him to admit how he was controlling patients.'

'A trap for the rat,' Wyatt interjected. 'Very daring for an untrained girl like Wendy. Do you think she can pull something like that off?'

Nash grinned. 'You remember back to how my little sister used to pretend she was on stage, playing theater when she was younger.'

'She always had a nice singing voice too,' Wyatt replied. 'Not so good as Brett's wife, Desiree. Now there's a lady who is a real songbird.'

'So, how was your trip? Martin asked. 'Did anyone try to stop you?'

Wyatt told him of the attempted ambush and Jared being on the trail of the remaining bushwhackers.

'I would have felt terrible if any of your family had been hurt or killed,' Trina told Martin.

'Our precaution and preparation paid off,' Wyatt said. 'We not only prevented those men from killing anyone, we eliminated five of them from doing harm to anyone else.'

'The folks will be proud,' Martin said.

Wyatt added, 'Jared won't let the others get away.

Soon as we get Miss Barrett square with the law, I intend to join him in the hunt.'

'You Valerons – all of you – have been so wonderful.' Tears glistened in Trina's eyes. 'I don't know how to ever thank you.'

'We've still got your freedom to win,' Martin said. 'Let's save the thanks until we've finished the job.'

'Speaking of jobs,' Dizzy slipped into their conversation, 'I wonder if any of you would be willing to act as my assistant. I have some testing to do yet, and the people I have hired all quit after the first day.'

'Human test subjects are rather hard to find,' Nash remarked. 'Maybe you could try prisoners, those who are behind bars and serving twenty years to life.'

'Yeah,' Martin agreed, 'a person with nothing to live for might be just what you need. You could offer to help them escape their shackles by living in a dream world.'

'That's a brilliant idea!' Dizzy exclaimed. 'I wonder if the Governor would go along with it?'

Trina took hold of Nash's hand and squeezed it. As she had his attention, she asked Martin, 'Is this plan of yours going to work? I mean, if Wendy can testify about the doctor, would that mean the judge would set me free?'

Martin gave her a confident smile. 'Don't worry, Trina. You've got all of us on your side; we won't let anyone put you back in that place.'

'How long before Wendy is back from the meeting?' Wyatt wanted to know.

'She might be at her room already,' Martin replied. 'We were just headed over to see how things went. Come on, let's go.'

Everyone filed out of the apartment, but Trina held Nash back. As soon as they were alone, she threw her arms around his neck and clung to him.

'Nash,' she murmured. 'I can't help it. I'm so afraid!'

'I know,' he said gently. 'It's going to be very hard on you, having to face the doctor at the hearing tomorrow. But you have to stay strong. We are all here to help, and we are going to see justice is done.'

She pulled back to look at him, but looking was not enough. Her lips were suddenly on his and he found her kiss soft, moist and wonderful!

Turk, who was taking the first shift of night watch, heard Callisto arrive. The yard man also tended the animals. He took the horse to put it away and the doctor entered the waiting room. The big man grinned, seeing him in the fancy suit of clothes.

'What do you think, boss? We gonna have another sheep to add to the flock?'

Callisto loosened his collar and his face worked with his turning over of different thoughts. 'Did Manny get back from town yet?'

'Trina come in on the train,' he related to him. 'Manny come by after you had left for Denver. He said she was traveling with some guy – looked like a jack-leg lawyer or something. Certainly not a gun hand. Trina and the guy went to a private office for a bit, then they both got rooms at the hotel.'

'A private office? That of a lawyer?'

'No, some nothing apartment where a nutty character

named Delacruz lives. Don't know what he does to earn a living.' Turk, seeing the troubled look on Callisto's face, asked, 'Does that mean something to you, boss?'

The doctor put a hand over his stomach. 'Um, something on the menu tonight didn't set very well. Perhaps it's nerves.'

'What about the new client?'

'I don't know. She was attractive and quite charming.'

'So?' Turk continued to pry. 'What's the problem?'

'There is something very disturbing about the timing of Mrs Vandermeer's arrival. She just happens to want to get rid of an abusive husband the night before Trina's hearing. It might be a coincidence, but it might not.'

'You believe the lady tonight was counterfeit, like maybe some kind of trick?'

'I think we need to be very cautious. Lucile said her son would take care of Trina, that she would never arrive, yet we know she is in a Denver hotel this very minute. What could have happened?'

'Manny took a fresh horse and returned to keep an eye on her,' Turk said. 'You want that I should ride to town and see the girl has an accident tonight?'

'It's already after ten, and I have to make the trip back to town early tomorrow. There isn't much time to do anything.'

'I could make time,' Turk said, his features dark and significant. 'Me and Manny could slip in there and do the job. Just give me some of that special potion you keep around. It worked on Mr Barrett – ought to do the same for his daughter.'

Callisto pondered the options. He would testify the

girl had bouts of depression and suffered from fits and loss of mental faculties. But the girl's system would be free of any drug by this time. She might win the favor of the judge . . . especially if she had herself a smart lawyer. And if Mrs Vandermeer had been sent in as a decoy to incriminate him, she would testify he had offered to make her husband look crazy. The risk was great; everything was at stake.

'I'll follow the schedule as if I expect her to attend the hearing,' he explained to Turk. Then he walked through to his office, opened the medicine cabinet and retrieved a small bottle. Turk had followed him, so he handed over the container.

'Give this to her,' he said. 'Try to hide any signs of forcing her to drink it. We want it to look as if she had an apoplexy during the night. Don't let anyone see you.'

'We'll take care of it, boss.'

'You and Manny can expect a nice bonus this month,' Callisto told him. 'I'll hire an extra man for nights, and you two will only have to fill in once a week for his day off.'

'This is the safest way to deal with Trina.' Turk flashed a sinister grin. 'Bet that witch, Lucile, will agree. She should fork over a handsome payment for this little accident.'

'I'm sure she will.'

CHAPTER EIGHT

Wyatt, Dodge and Reb rented a room with two bunks at the hotel. They didn't need a third, as each of them was to take a three hour shift to keep watch during the night. As Martin and Trina already had rooms with two beds, Nash joined Martin and Wendy shared Trina's room. It should have been a safe enough arrangement, but three of the ambushers had escaped. They also had to be wary of a secondary plan to prevent the girl from attending the court hearing. First rule of protection: vigilance.

Wyatt turned over the watch assignment to Dodge at midnight. He told him there was a good place across the street by a Farmer's Implement supply store. Some rain barrels were displayed in front which allowed a man to sit in near total darkness and keep watch of the hotel entrance. From the corner of the building, it was possible to also see the back door of the rooming house at the same time.

Dodge was comfortably resting on an empty drum, with his back against the facade of the building, deep in the shadows. He sat up straight when he saw two men approach the hotel. One was a rather large bruiser and the other was a squat-built Mexican. They appeared nervous, looking around more than a normal person would. Bruiser entered and approached the desk. He spoke to the clerk and the hotel employee went into a back room. Soon as he had left the counter, Bruiser reached over and pulled the sign-in register around to examine it. He pushed it back where it had been as the clerk returned with a candle.

'So you needed a candle and the stores are closed,' Dodge mumbled under his breath. 'Nice move to get a look at the guests and their room numbers.'

Even as he kept watch, the Mexican vanished down the alleyway as far as the rear exit. He returned almost immediately and waited near the door for his pal.

Bruiser thanked the clerk and flipped him a coin for the penny-candle and his courtesy. Then he left the hotel and joined up with the Mexican.

There were a few people on the streets, most heading home for the night. A number of gas lamps glowed along the main streets, but there were shadows and dark alleys aplenty. Bruiser and Mex wandered down the street. To anyone who saw them, it appeared they were ambling off to one of the saloons or late-night taverns.

Turk and Manny stayed at a saloon until it closed. After that, they spent another hour sitting quietly in the darkness. It was cool, but not uncomfortable for early fall. Once enough time had passed, they used the secondary streets and alleyways to weave their way through the darkness to the hotel. It was the wee hours, a little before two in the morning, so the avenues were deserted and only the primary gas lamps were burning. A few buildings had night lights – a bank, a pharmacy that also offered jewelry, and the hotel lobby. Even the occasional dog had stopped barking for the night.

The two of them reached the rear access to the building and eased open the door. Before going inside, Turk struck a match and lit the candle. Then they entered quietly and gently closed the door behind them.

'Second floor,' Turk whispered. 'Should be the last room on the left. Remember,' he warned, 'no noise. We keep her from making a sound and force her to drink. Doc says it only takes a minute or two before this here medicine silences her for good.'

'Must be potent stuff,' Manny observed softly.

Turk led the way, using his cupped hand to prevent the candle from being blown out, while also limiting the amount of light it put off. They reached the top of the stairs and Manny tested the door.

'Locked!' he said in a hushed voice.

Turk used the light from the candle and slipped an ice pick into the lock. He was the product of a rather unsavory family, having spent much of his youth locked up for petty crimes. Breaking into a home or business was something he had learned from his older brother.

The door lock clicked and the knob turned. He and Manny remained perfectly still, both of them listening intently. After a few seconds, they assumed the slight noise had not awakened the girl inside.

Turk slipped the ice pick back in his belt so he could

use his free hand to hide the light from the candle. He gave Manny a nod and his partner pushed the door open ever so slowly, both of them wary of any squeaking sounds. A plush hotel like this one used a light coating of oil to maintain the hinges. There was only a mere whisper as the door opened.

Stepping inside, Turk kept the candle mostly covered, but a glimmer of light from a nearby street lamp penetrated the curtain of the cubicle's single window, making the interior minutely visible. The rooms on this floor all had one or two beds and a single closet. The second bunk was empty. Turk nodded to Manny and they approached the occupied bed. He produced the bottle of liquid. Once they had the girl subdued, he would be ready to force the medicine down her throat.

They reached the bed together. The sleeping form had a blanket covering her head. Manny leaned close and whispered, 'Hey, there, sweetheart. The sandman wants to help you sleep.' He reached out and yanked back the covers—

A gun suddenly appeared – shoved right up in his face!

'You ain't no sandman,' Reb snarled the words. 'And I ain't your sweetheart!'

'Don't move!' Wyatt commanded an icy warning, having come out of the closet. 'Hate to wake up the other hotel guests by shooting holes in you two!'

Reb got out of the bed as Dodge entered the room, having been discreetly watching them from down the hallway.

'Good thing we traded rooms with Nash's honey and Wendy,' Dodge said, pausing to light the lamp on the wall. Then he moved forward to disarm the pair, including the removal of the ice pick. He took the tiny bottle from them and passed it to Wyatt. Next, he removed two lengths of rawhide from his back pocket and bound the two intruders' hands behind their backs.

Taking no chances, Reb continued to hold a gun on the two men.

Once they were bound securely, and with enough light to see by, Wyatt opened the lid and examined the contents of the bottle. Looking at the pair, he said, 'if my cousin, Jared, was here, he'd demand we take you down to the stable and hang you both.'

'Manny and me must have come to the wrong room,' the large brute tried to explain their presence. 'We thought we was surprising a pal of ours. We were going to have some fun with him.'

'And this stuff in the bottle is what – some kind of potion to make him happy or drunk maybe?'

'Yeah,' Manny said. 'That's sure 'nuff what me and Turk had in mind. The stuff in the bottle is harmless.'

'So which one of you is going to drink this special potion?' Wyatt challenged. 'Let's see what kind of fun you were going to have with this friend of yours.'

Both of them paled in the dim light.

'I say we give them each half!' Dodge suggested. 'Be twice the entertainment that way.'

Wyatt held the bottle to the large man's lips. 'You first, Turk. Take a swig of this, but leave some for your pal.'

He sealed his lips tightly and shook his head.

'No?' Wyatt feigned amazement. 'But it's only a harmless drink to make a person feel happy or drunk. That's what you claimed, isn't it?'

'Mayhaps we ought to shove it down their throats,' Reb suggested. 'You know, it's what they were going to do to Miss Barrett. Let's see how much they like being on the receiving end of this here harmless prank!'

'I'll pinch Turk's nose until he has to take a breath,' Dodge volunteered. 'Reb, you pour the potion down his throat when he does.'

As Dodge wrapped an arm around Turk's neck and prepared to block his breathing with his free hand, the man blurted out, 'No! Wait! It's poison! We were supposed to give it to the girl. It would have looked like she died in her sleep.'

Dodge released his hold on the man. 'What do we do with them, Wyatt?'

'Reb, you go get Dizzy out of bed. Meet us over at the police headquarters – we passed it on the way into town.'

'I remember,' Reb replied. 'See you there in a few minutes.'

'Dodge, knock on Martin's door. Let my brother and Nash know what we're doing. Soon as we get these jaspers to the police station, you slip back up here and keep watch. It ought to be safe enough for the night, but we'll stay alert.'

'Right,' Dodge said, then hurried to obey. He left the room just long enough to speak to the two Valerons. When he returned, Wyatt and he marched their prisoners out of the hotel.

*

With his horse on a lead rope following, Robby used a buggy to drive his mother from the ranch to Restful Acres to collect the doctor. When Callisto came out to meet them, it was obvious something was amiss.

'What is it?' Lucile asked at once. 'You look like you've been up all night.'

The doctor appeared haggard from lack of sleep, but there was also a wildness in the stringency of his face and an overall unkempt look about him. He hadn't shaved, so the dark stubble covered the area around his usually neatly trimmed mustache. Dark circles were under his eyes and he seemed quite flushed, as if he had a fever. Even as Robby got down and the doctor climbed aboard the carriage, Callisto paused to search the grounds, whipping his head about this way and that.

'Someone is watching!' Callisto quivered, holding his breath. 'I feel it.'

Lucile took a quick survey of the area and scowled at him. 'You're losing your poise, Doctor. There's nobody out here but us.'

'What's wrong?' Robby wanted to know, having retrieved his mount. 'Are you hiding something from us?'

Callisto shook his head. 'No. I mean . . . I can't say. It's just that. . . .'

'That what?' Lucile snapped impatiently. 'What's gotten into you?'

'Turk and Manny,' he finally blundered forth the story. 'They should have been back hours ago.'

115

'What are you talking about, Doctor?' Robby commanded. 'Where did they go?'

Callisto rattled on with a complicated explanation of how his two men were supposed to give Trina a drug to induce heart failure. He had kept a man in town to watch the train and Trina was seen arriving with some man. They knew she was staying at the hotel. Turk and Manny were to get rid of her and put an end to their problems.

'But they haven't returned!' he finished, his voice shrill, like that of a frightened child. 'It's all wrong. Everything is wrong!'

'What do you think, Mother?' Robby asked, still holding the lead rope to his horse.

Lucile's lips pressed tightly together. 'I think,' she said earnestly, 'you ought to do what we spoke of. Wait at the Meadows' trading post until you hear from me.'

'You want me to leave without you?'

'They have no proof of anything. Dr Callisto will testify how Trina broke down after her father's death. Even if the judge rules in her favor, there is nothing they can charge me with.'

'So why should I run?'

'Because of the failed attempt by your old outlaw pals – the attack that *didn't* stop Trina from getting back for the hearing. If they took one of those men alive, and he talked, they might charge you as an accessory to the ambush.'

'But—'

She held up a hand to prevent further argument. 'If nothing comes of all this, I will meet you later. If Trina

116

is deemed competent, I'm sure she will want us both gone from the ranch. So long as you're out of the reach of the law and have the money we need to start over, I will come to join you.'

Robby obviously didn't like the plan, but his mother always knew what was best. He climbed aboard his mare, told her farewell, and turned the horse for the ranch. He would pick up the belongings that were already packed, along with the money they had stashed. It was risky, but he figured Breed would be willing to listen to his story. Nothing talked a more convincing language than money – if he offered the gang leader enough of it. Considering the ambush had not worked, and he had lost several men, he should be satisfied to get paid the balance of what had been promised.

The hearing began with Trina and Martin sitting at one table, while Lucile, Callisto, and a local lawyer were at a second. Oddly, the judge bid Callisto testify before the court first.

'Dr Callisto,' the judge began. 'It has come to light that you have been using drugs from a variety of plants to control your subjects.'

'Uh, what's that?' he asked inanely. 'I did what?'

'Mr Delacruz, a well-established researcher in the field of plants and botany, has suggested you are controlling your patients with drugs from toxic plants. He has produced a sample of your medication for this court.' The judge held up a small bottle. 'It is a potion you provided for two of your men. They were to use it on Miss Barrett to prevent her testimony here today.'

'My men?' Callisto muttered. 'I don't understand. What is going on here? Why are you blaming me? I've done nothing wrong.'

'Do you employ Jeb Turkleson and Manny Degorio at your facility known as Restful Acres?'

'Uh . . . well, yeah.'

'They were caught in a hotel room rented out to Miss Barrett last night. The two of them had this bottle of medicine you gave them, and had orders to force her to drink it. Mr Delacruz has identified the contents of this vessel as a deadly poison. Her death would have looked exactly like that of her father.'

'I knew it!' Callisto cried. 'You're out to get me! Everyone is after me!'

'Do you admit to giving this bottle of liquid to your two hired men?'

'Hired men?' he looked dumbly around. 'What hired men? I don't know what you're talking about!' He became frantic. 'Who have you had watching me? What are you looking for?'

'Calm down, Dr Callisto,' the judge warned. 'You are making a scene.'

'But I'm innocent!' he cried. 'Besides, I only do what I can to help people! I provide a service to the community.'

'You mean helping people who wish to be rid of someone?' the judge enquired.

'Yes!' he blurted. Then he thought better of it. 'I mean – no! It isn't. . . .' But he couldn't get his mouth to form the needed words. Instead, he bolted from the chair and made a dash for the door. Two policemen

118

were there to block his escape. They subdued him with little effort and dragged him back to stand in front of the judge.

'Are you familiar with Jimsonweed and belladonna?' the judge asked him. 'Because you ingested a small portion of the extract from those two plants last night.'

'What?!' Callisto was shocked. 'I'm sick!' he declared. 'Consuming that kind of drug, I might fall into delirium, or begin to blather like an idiot.'

'You mean like Miss Barrett did at her sanity hearing last year?'

'Huh?' The doctor struggled against the police officers on either side, both holding tightly to his arms. 'You can't . . . I mean, I was only doing what I was hired to. . . .'

'Shut up!' Lucile shouted at him, rising to her feet. 'You incompetent imbecile! Keep your stupid mouth shut!'

'Would you care to add something, Mrs Gowan-Barrett?' the judge asked politely. 'I was going to give you a chance to speak, when you were formally charged with the murder of your husband and the attempted murder of your stepdaughter. But go ahead, say your piece.'

The lawyer grabbed her arm and forcibly made her sit down. Lucile's face flamed red with ire and humiliation. Her teeth were bared like a snarling dog, but she kept her jaw tightly clenched and said nothing more.

'Take them away,' the judge ordered the two policemen. 'I will hear the formal charges once the district attorney has had time to finish your investigation.'

119

'Your Honor,' the lawyer tried to speak. 'I must insist that you release my client! This hearing has been a mockery of justice.'

'Yes,' the judge replied. 'There has been a mockery of justice – and I intend to set the record straight. Save your indignation for the trial.'

The lawyer walked silently behind both Callisto and Lucile, as they were led from the room amid a few cat-calls and insults, thrown at them from the people who had come to the hearing. Once they were gone, the judge tapped his gavel to silence the audience.

'Miss Barrett,' he directed his words to the young lady. 'I offer you my sincerest apology for what you have suffered. I assure you, we will look into the lives of the other patients confined at Restful Acres, as well as pursue a line of prosecution for the guilty parties in the attacks on your person and the death of your father. I humbly dismiss all claims concerning your mental competency from the court's previous findings. You are a free woman.' He then offered a singular smile. 'Court dismissed.'

CHAPTER NINE

'I'm sure of it,' Lobo told Kidd and Breed. 'I've been hanging back, keeping watch the whole blasted day! The guy is very good, but I finally caught a glimpse of him when he had to cross an open patch of ground. He's dead on our tracks.'

'Valeron!' Breed declared. 'Damn! He must have the nose of a bloodhound.'

'Soon as we make the turn toward Robby's ranch, he will know our direction and can get ahead of us,' Lobo worried.

Kidd frowned. 'You think he knows about Robby?'

'How else could anyone have known about our ambush?' Breed spoke up. 'They knew where we were going to attack and suckered us with a couple dummies in a wagon.'

'Well, if he's the same joker who killed Mont and the Pratts, he's deadly with a rifle. If he was to circle ahead and lie in wait, he could kill two of us before we had a chance to find cover.'

'We could set a trap for him,' Breed said, mostly

talking to himself. 'But whoever the man is, he is probably on the lookout for something like that.'

'Like I said,' Lobo added to his conclusion, 'I almost didn't see him on our back trail. The man's a ghost. If he guessed we were going to bushwhack him, he might work around and maybe get the drop on us.'

'Don't care for our chances when you put it in that light,' Kidd said. 'If we try to ambush him, he kills a couple of us – if he gets ahead of us, he kills a couple of us. Got to be a third choice!'

Breed was silent, his mind working, seeking options. Finally, he uttered a dejected sigh. 'All right. We are going to head for Robby's ranch – say, ride that way until an hour or two before dark. Then we'll cut back around and make for the Meadows' trading post.'

'You don't think Robby will show up with our payment, do you?' Kidd asked.

'He might, if he's running. Whatever reason he had for us to get rid of that girl, it failed. He could be in the same fix as we are.'

'Our tracker will still be on our tail,' Lobo said.

'Yeah, but he'll be confused by our change of direction. If we play our cards right, he will figure we have decided no one is after us. He only has to get careless for a short way and we will put as many holes in him as we did the dummies in the buggy.'

'I like it,' Kidd approved. 'If he's dumb or stubborn enough to keep following us, he'll be riding straight to a shallow grave.'

'Let's go,' Lobo said. 'I'm sore as hell from this gunshot wound and could use a good night's sleep.'

'If he tries to overtake us, we'll have him. If he doesn't take the bait, Kidd and I will take the watch tonight,' Breed outlined. 'Lobo, you can catch up on your sleep and heal up a little.'

'I'd rather our shadow was dead,' Lobo said. 'I don't trust that phantom – not one damn bit.'

With Turk and Manny making statements, Lucile and the doctor were both held for one count of murder and the attempted murder of Trina. The doctor also faced a host of charges for drugging and holding people captive. A warrant was issued for Robby Gowan and Dizzy made a visit to Restful Acres with two policemen and a nurse from the hospital. Zelda would be arrested for her part in the incarceration of drugged patients and any groundskeepers, cooks or other personnel would be terminated. Callisto was out of business.

Martin and Wendy joined Trina and the others on the trip out to the Barrett ranch. Martin would go over the accounting books, while Dodge and Reb would work with the wranglers and cowhands to determine how many cattle and horses were still on the place.

Nash and Trina rode in the carriage that Callisto and Lucile had come to town in. After all, it belonged to the ranch. With two wagons and three riders, they left Denver like a small cavalcade. However, Wyatt and the two ranch hands rode on ahead, in case Robby was still on the ranch.

For Trina, this was the beginning of the end to her

association with the Valerons. She was returning to what rightfully belonged to her, going back to a life she had known before the death of her father. Why then did she not revel at the prospect?

'I feel relieved,' Trina spoke up after they had traveled several miles. 'But,' she cast a sidelong glance at Nash, 'I am also quite lost.'

He continued to stare straight ahead, having been uncomfortably silent to this point.

'You have your ranch back,' he said finally, withholding any outward emotion. 'Martin will get your finances in order, and no one knows cattle better than Reb and Dodge. A day or two with the ranch help and everything will be back to normal.'

'Will you stay at the ranch?' she asked. 'I mean, for a day or two?'

'I can't ignore my practice,' he replied. 'Barely open a month and I'm closed down for a week. I hate to do that to the people who are going to rely on my services in the future.'

'The ranch was my father's legacy,' Trina mused. 'He built it up from a one-room shack and a dozen cattle. My mother and I, we all about starved when I was little, barely eking out a living. If my father hadn't left with a couple other men to round up wild range cattle after the end of the War between the Union and the Confederacy, we would have gone broke.'

'I was a teenager back then,' Nash said. 'I remember my dad and two uncles doing much the same thing. They rounded up wild horses and cattle to add to our herds.'

'When Dad had our house built, it was like moving into a mansion. I had my own room, we had a pump in the house, store-bought beds and furniture . . . it was like a dream come true.'

'My time was spent reading books and studying to become a doctor,' Nash confided to her. 'I never wanted to be anything else.'

'I can see why,' Trina said. 'When you operated on that young girl and removed her appendix, it was so amazing, so gratifying. To see her smile, after having been in such pain – it was like a miracle.'

He cocked his head to the side enough to smile at her. 'I couldn't have done it without you. If you hadn't held the incision open, while I removed and tied it off, the appendix might have burst and she would have died. I didn't save her life – *we* saved her life.'

'What will you do for a nurse?' she asked. 'Wendy told me she was going back home. Her revulsion to blood is not something she can overcome.'

'All people are not cut out to deal with the blood, broken bones and suffering of the ill or injured. The same can be said for most any other profession. I could never do the intense paperwork and endless figures that Martin does. He grew up loving numbers, Jared hunted mice and sage hens with a slingshot, before he had a gun. Brett always wanted to be a lawman – and so on. Each person, given the opportunity, has a field they enjoy or do well in. For some, like another of my cousins, Shane, his passion is horses. Wendy has a wonderful wit and can charm or talk to anyone. She will find her way to something she enjoys one day.'

'I don't especially care for cattle or living on a ranch,' Trina confessed. 'I've never been like one of your family – you know, able to think of myself and what I wanted. I acted as expected, like most other children of ranchers or farmers. I did my chores and helped with whatever was needed.'

'Few people have the choices I had,' Nash said. 'I realize how fortunate I have been. It isn't. . . '

A rider appeared on the trail coming fast. Nash pulled back on the reins as he recognized Dodge. Martin and Wendy pulled their rig up alongside to see why Nash had stopped. The four of them watched as the man continued to close distance at a gallop, eventually pulling his horse to a stop in front of the carriage.

'Robby is gone!' he announced, panting from the hard ride. 'The fellow who tends the yard said he left early this morning. Had a fair amount of belongings with him, as if he was going to be gone for a spell.'

'Must have guessed we would win the court hearing,' Nash surmised.

Wendy gave a huff of contempt. 'The dirty little rat! He pulled out before the law could come after him.'

Dodge spoke again. 'The yard keeper says the Gowans sold a hundred head of cattle a few weeks back. He thought it odd, considering the price of beef is pretty low this time of year.'

'Money to hire a band of killers,' Nash made a deduction. 'What is Wyatt going to do?'

'Already done it,' Dodge informed him. 'He took some supplies and traded for a fresh horse. He's on Robby's trail.'

'I wouldn't want to be Robby Gowan right now,' Wendy quipped. 'He's going to wish he had given himself up to the law!'

'How about you and Reb?' Martin asked.

'We'll stick for a bit,' Dodge confirmed. 'You done give us the task of counting cattle and taking a close look at the lady's hired help. We intend to remove any culls afore we leave her on her own.'

'All right,' Nash said. 'Let's get on to the ranch. We've got a lot of work to do.'

'I'll ride along with you,' Dodge said. 'Gave my hoss quite a workout riding here like I did.'

'We appreciate your coming to let us know what was going on,' Martin spoke from the next carriage. 'Won't be any surprises that way.'

As the small procession began to move again, Trina reached over and placed her hand on Nash's arm. He transferred his reins to one hand and placed his other over her own.

'See?' he encouraged her. 'Everything is working out as planned. You'll soon have your ranch back in operation and be the queen of your own little empire.'

'I can never repay you for what you've done for me,' she murmured softly, 'your whole family, Nash.'

He turned his head enough to look at her, deeply moved by the gentleness and beauty of the woman. She had suffered so much, yet looked as innocent and sweet as a newborn baby. The thought of leaving her caused his heart to swell in his chest. Swallowing seemed impossible due to the lump lodged in his throat.

Say something, stupid! His brain scolded him. *Don't*

127

let this moment slip away!

Trina suddenly pulled her hand away, returning her attention to the road ahead. Nash thought he saw a slight hesitation, a moment when tears had begun to glisten in her eyes. Was she overcome with emotion too? Or had Nash only imagined it? Either way, the perfect opportunity to tell her how he felt had slipped away.

Jared studied the ground, still puzzled by the latest change of direction. The trio of outlaws had made a direct line for a point near Denver. He had an approximate idea of where Trina's ranch was located. It was a route that made sense. They were going to join up with Robby Gowan. But now, a couple hours before dusk, they had completely reversed their direction.

He rose up in his stirrups and stared off at their new path. There were miles and miles of open land, full of choppy hills and tree- and brush-covered terrain. He knew of no towns or settlements of any size in the distance.

Jared went to his saddle-bags and removed his field glasses. If this was a plan to trap him, he would have to be doubly cautious. Were they making a run for a hideout or luring him into a narrow canyon or place where they could launch a sneak attack and kill him?

After a lengthy survey of the area, he finally spotted three dots on the horizon, catching sight of his prey as they topped a rise a couple of miles away. It helped to know where they were, as he could leave their trail and circle far enough to one side to avoid any ambush. But it also caused him concern. This was mostly new territory to him. He had traveled through various places during his hunts into the Dakotas, but he didn't know the smaller settlements or trading posts that might be along the trail in different directions.

As a hunter, Jared enjoyed being alone. A solitary huntsman could move with a greater degree of quiet, listening to the sounds around him, unfettered by a companion who might make a noise or speak at the wrong time. Wild game had come to know the sound of men and were easily spooked. The game he played presently was life or death between him and three other men. He didn't need anyone giving away his location with a cough, sneeze or stepping on a stick and alerting his quarry. However, he had no help in a fight, no one to share the night watch with or offer a second opinion.

Allowing his horse a breather, he considered his options. He could close the distance between him and the three men, or he could play it safe. Exposing themselves at the crest of a hill seemed a greenhorn mistake, considering all of the different ways the outlaws had been trying to cover their tracks and lose any pursuit.

'You boys know I'm here, don't you?' Jared said softly. 'You were hoping I'd see you ride boldly over the hill, as if you hadn't a worry in the world.'

His heart began to pound with anticipation. If the idea had been to show themselves, they would manifestly set a trap for him. Once out of his sight, they would probably split up and take positions to catch him in a crossfire as he appeared over the very same hill.

On the other hand, if they didn't know he was behind them, this was a chance to gain ground on them. He might get within shooting distance if he pushed his horse for the next hour or two. He needed to make the right decision.

The evening meal was prepared by the cook and cleaning lady Lucile had hired. Mildred was in her late forties and had been a widow for several years. Her only daughter had married, so she was alone, destitute, and her previous livelihood had been earned by cleaning a saloon in town and sleeping in a storeroom. She was a passable cook and Trina offered to keep her on . . . with an increase in wages.

'Seems an able woman,' Martin remarked to Trina, after the table had been cleared after dinner.

'Yes, Mildred said her only daughter had married a carpenter's helper. They had a child on the way and could barely keep a roof over their heads. She didn't want to be a burden to them, so she has been doing what she could to get by.'

'We've a few people working for us at the ranch or in Valeron who suffered similar conditions,' Martin told her.

'Uh,' Reb spoke up. 'Me and Dodge got a lot of riding to do tomorrow, Miss Barrett. If you don't mind, we'll sashay out to the bunkhouse and find a bed for the night.'

'Certainly,' she said. 'You men have been like guardian angels. I don't know how I could have managed without you.'

Reb gave her an ah shucks sort of smile, and he and Dodge left the table. Martin and Nash remained seated, as there were still some things to be sorted out. Wendy had offered to help with the dishes, so she was in the kitchen with Mildred.

'They said you have several able men working the herd, and the Dutchman – as he likes to be called – handles most of the chores around the ranch house.'

'I offered him the choice of eating with us, but he prefers to take his meals with Mildred.'

'They are about the same age,' Martin noted. 'Could be they enjoy each other's company.'

'Tell her what you've found, Martin,' Nash spoke for the first time. He had been taciturn since their arrival at the ranch, staying mostly with Martin and helping where he could.

'The journal has been kept up to date, Miss Barrett. Because your father's will left everything to you, they couldn't withdraw any unauthorized funds from the bank. It was what forced them to sell some of the livestock – twenty-five of the horses the first month you were imprisoned at Restful Acres and then a hundred head of prime beef a short time ago. Otherwise, your mortgage payment and monthly payroll were paid by the bank. That much was covered in your father's will.'

Martin paused from the summation and gave her a solemn look. 'I'm real sorry you lost your pa. He seemed to have cared about you deeply, and he had a good head on his shoulders. It's too bad he couldn't have found a way to be rid of Lucile, before she managed to poison him.'

'I'm sure he had come to realize the kind of gold-grubber Lucile was, and he never did like Robby. He predicted he would end up in prison or at the end of a rope.'

'Wyatt will bring him back alive,' Nash declared. 'Unless Robby is fool enough to try and shoot it out with him.'

'Well, Miss Barrett.' Martin got back to business. 'I don't see any need for me and Wendy to stay any longer. She is eager to get back home, and I'm equally anxious to see my wife and kids. I thought we might leave early tomorrow so we can catch the train as far as Cheyenne.'

'By all means!' she approved. 'You've been wonderful – both of you!'

'Then I'll turn in for the night.'

'Dutch can ready the carriage for the two of you. Were you going to stay for breakfast?'

'According to the train schedule, we need to be there early. Wendy and I will have our meal in town, before we board.'

He walked around and took her hand in a farewell gesture. 'I'll tell Wendy, so she is up and ready – likely a little before daybreak. We should leave at first light.'

Nash stood up. 'I guess I'll call it a night too. Been a long day.'

Trina regarded him with an apprehensive mien. 'You're not leaving?' Hearing the desperation in her voice, she quickly added, 'I mean, you said you would stay until everything was settled.'

Nash hesitated, so Martin answered in his place. 'We need to have someone here until we hear back from Wyatt or Jared. I'm sure Nash can manage another day or two.'

'Yes,' Nash said, having been forced to commit. 'I suppose my practice can wait a little longer.'

'Especially since you are making money on this trip, huh?' Martin reminded him. 'Wyatt said he was forwarding the bounty for those bandits. That'll earn you more than six months of actual paying customers from Castle Point.'

'It will help cover a lot of expenses,' Nash agreed.

Then the two Valerons left the room and Trina joined Wendy and Mildred in the kitchen. They had finished up and Mildred was enquiring about the time and number there would be for breakfast.

'It will just be four for breakfast,' Trina informed her. 'Nash and the two Valeron hands will eat with me. You can serve the others as usual.'

'Two are staying with the herd,' Mildred informed her, 'so it's only me, Dutch and the other two regular hands. I will serve them at six and have the main house meal ready at seven.'

'You are worth twice what I offered to pay you,' Trina praised her.

'Nonsense, Miss Barrett, I am happy to be useful again. Working for you will be a pleasure, after Lucile and her spoiled brat son. They were very demanding.'

Trina said goodnight to Mildred and she left.

'I'm going to miss you,' Trina spoke to Wendy once they were alone. 'You are the kind of friend I never had growing up. Being an only child, I pretty much did everything alone.'

Wendy laughed. 'I never got to be alone. Four older brothers and an older sister in the house, along with a bunch of cousins from my two uncles' families next door.'

The two of them walked into the sitting room and took a seat on the couch. Wendy was intuitive enough to know Trina wanted to say something important. When she was slow to speak, Wendy did what she always did – she started a serious conversation.

'So.' She peered intently at Trina. 'What are you going to do about Nash?'

Trina blinked in surprise, not ready for such a direct question. 'I . . . I don't know what you mean.'

'Come now, girlfriend,' Wendy delivered the line in a teasing manner. 'There are stars in your eyes every time you look at him. It's as obvious as the nose on your face.'

'Gadfry!' she exclaimed. 'You don't beat about the bush, do you?'

'Sisters or girlfriends don't skirt the issues,' Wendy advised her. 'It's best to share everything . . . except the same man.'

'I usually kept to myself,' Trina admitted. 'I don't know the rules about girlfriends.'

Wendy laughed. 'We make them up as we go along – drives the guys crazy! They never have a clue as to what we're thinking!'

'You seem to know what's on my mind.'

'I believe you and Nash are made for each other – except for living so far apart.'

Trina sighed. 'I tried to speak to him, but. . . .' She lifted her shoulders and let them fall.

'Nash is an extraordinary catch,' Wendy said. 'And he needs a nurse to help with his work. Look how great you two were together! Why, you and he saved that little girl as if you had been working together for years. And you are wonderful with the patients.'

'But I have this ranch to run,' Trina argued. 'My father built it up from nothing. It was his legacy.'

Wendy stuck out a finger and tapped Trina on the breastbone. 'You are his legacy, Trina. If he's the wonderful guy you make him out to be, he'd want what is best for you – what would make you the most happy.'

'But Nash. . . .' She struggled to find the words. 'Well, he did mention courting, and we did share a kiss – but that was before the hearing. He hasn't made any advances since. What am I supposed to do?'

Wendy waved a careless hand. 'Nash is bashful and lacks experience in wooing a girl. Besides which, like some men, he doesn't know what's best for him.'

'And you do?'

Wendy smiled. 'You bet I do! And I can tell you, *you* are what he wants.'

Trina wrung her hands, her emotions washing about inside of her like the ocean waves slapping up against the shore. She wanted to believe Wendy, but she was as inexperienced as Nash, when it came to romance.

'Listen to me,' Wendy confided, 'Nash is probably suffering the assumption that you are in love with this ranch, and he can't give up his practice. If you want him, you have to let him know that he means more to you than this house and a handful of cattle.'

'You expect me to what? Throw myself at him?'

Wendy laughed. 'Yes. Go for it! He'll catch you.'

'And what if he doesn't?'

'Trust me, Trina.' Wendy grew deadly serious. 'Nash would fail miserably if he tried to tell you how much he loves you . . . but I know he does.'

'How can you be so sure?'

'I've seen the way he looks at you . . . usually when you aren't aware of it. I know my brother, and you should heed my advice. Don't let him get away. You would both regret it for the rest of your lives.'

'I wish you weren't leaving tomorrow,' Trina said. 'I could use your support.'

'Just flutter your eyes, lean in close enough that he can feel your breath on his cheek, then tell him you don't want him to leave.'

Trina lowered her head, feeling a tremendous heat flood up into her face, and that was only a reaction to Wendy's suggestion. How would she ever manage to do the real thing?

'Here.' Wendy handed her a piece of paper. 'If everything else fails, I jotted this down for you. I guarantee it will work.'

Trina looked at what was written, then scowled at her. 'It's silly.'

'When you're in love, silly works,' Wendy replied.

'Thanks a lot, girlfriend,' she muttered cynically. 'I begin to see why men think women are such a mystery!'

CHAPTER TEN

Jared remained downwind and out of sight. He hadn't taken the bait, when the outlaws exposed themselves at the crest of the hill. Instead, he had circled their position and taken up a new vigil. He had waited them out for over an hour, before they decided he was either not following, or refused to walk into a trap. When they moved down the trail again, he did so too, but only when certain he would be undetected by the trio of ambushers. He hoped they would think they had lost him and relax for the night.

Shortly after the sun set, the group left the main trail. They chose a sheltered cove among trees and brush, enclosed by chaparral, which they expected would protect them from being discovered.

Jared staked out his horse, then ate a cold meal and bided his time, outlining his plan in his head. Two hours after full darkness, he carefully approached their encampment.

The gang's horses were tethered on a single line and the three men had laid out their beds in a rather large triangle. Jared waited patiently, making sure the camp was asleep – at least, two of the three outlaws. He anticipated the third man would be on night watch.

Had these men killed Nash or the girl, rather than a pair of dress forms, he would have had no compunction about charging in with his gun blazing and eliminated each one. However, one or more of them might be needed to testify against the person who hired the ambush. So Jared had thought out a plan to subdue and restrain three men, without risking a fight.

One thing worked to his advantage: the horses' picket line was also downwind of the camp. The location made it more difficult for the bandits to hear their animals. Horses often shifted their feet, stomped when a night fly would land on a sensitive part of their legs, or shake their manes and swat with their tails. Plus, horses had a habit of bickering with one another, each wanting their own space – and a few inches of their neighbors' space as well. An experienced man would listen to his animals and know when they were behaving normally, or when something else was going on. He would have to make the assumption these were all experienced men, so he was extra careful.

The lone guard moved once or twice, but the fool was smoking a cigarette, which gave away his position. Jared had stuffed a handful of oats into his jacket pocket and watched until the sentry walked to the far side of the camp. When he squatted down on a fallen log, it offered Jared the chance to put his plan into motion.

First task: Jared made a slow and easy approach toward the horses. Knowing the animals' hearing was more acute than a man's, he spoke softly as he drew closer, so they didn't spook. Once close to them, he patted each one and cooed appreciative words, keeping his voice hushed and amiable. As they accepted his presence, he moved to the one furthermost from the camp and fed him a handful of oats. Then he removed the lariat from a nearby saddle, untied the lead rope to that pony and led him silently away.

Second task: Jared waited until the man had been on duty for another hour, meaning it was probable the other two were sleeping soundly. Then, when the guard had his back to the slight breeze, Jared moved on his toes and closed the distance without disturbing the dust underfoot. He paused, fifteen feet away, staying in the deepest of shadows from the nearby brush and trees. At the appropriate moment – when the guard yawned mightily and stretched his arms out to the sides – Jared moved swiftly up behind him.

'Move. . . .' Jared hissed in a harsh whisper, slipping his hunting knife under his chin, 'and I'll cut your throat!'

He kept the knife in place, while using his free hand to secure the man's left arm behind him and halfway up his back. In such a position, he forced the man to back up slowly – step by step – until they were far enough from the two sleeping men to not be overheard.

Third task: The ambusher gave up his name and also the other two. Jared bound Kidd's hands behind him and placed him on the horse bareback. Next, he put a noose around the man's neck, cinched it snug, and secured the other end over a tree branch, pulling it tight enough that the man could hardly draw a breath.

'Now you can see the dilemma, Kidd,' Jared warned him. 'I didn't gag you, because the rope around your neck is strung up tight. It would only take a slight move-ment of your horse and you would be left dangling in the air.'

The outlaw glared through the gloom at him but said nothing.

'And I suppose you noticed that I have released your horse from his lead rope. He is free to walk away at any time. If he does. . . .' Jared gave him an impish grin. 'Well, you can guess what might happen, if you were brazen enough to yell a warning to the camp. This here steed might stand still, and he might not. If you wish to take the chance, by all means, call out to your pals.'

'You're crazy!' the outlaw said, though he kept his voice hushed.

'Better use your breath to coax your bronc to stand real still,' Jared told him. 'Sure hope you boys are riding well-trained animals. Hate to go to all this trouble for nothing.'

Kidd held his tongue, other than to whisper, 'Easy!' or 'whoa, fella!' or 'steady, boy!' to the horse under him.

Jared left him on his own good behavior and returned to the camp. Instead of taking a chance one of the men would wake up and wonder where Kidd was, or why he hadn't woken him, Jared donned the weather-worn hat Kidd had been wearing. He moved quietly and looked over the two men. His plan was to deal with one at a time, but which one? Even as he stood there, one of the pair groaned a little as he changed position. Doing so, the blanket uncovered his shirt enough that Jared saw his bandage. He decided to risk waking the other one.

Ever so gently, he used the toe of his boot to nudge the sleeping form. It took about three tries before the man turned over and looked up. Jared ducked his head so he would see Kidd's hat and not his face.

'My turn already?' the outlaw said softly. 'Damn, seems like I just closed my eyes.'

Jared grunted and pretended to move over to the empty bed, about twenty feet away. The relief guard got to his feet, and, when his back was turned, Jared disappeared into the darkness. When he looked back, the relief man hadn't paid any attention, picking up his rifle and walking quietly to the place where Kidd had been keeping watch.

Jared watched him for thirty minutes, then he repeated his plan. All three tasks went as smoothly as the first time. Once he had Breed on a horse next to Kidd, he gave an appreciative look at his handiwork.

'Good thing you boys carry ropes,' Jared told them. 'Otherwise, I'd have just hanged you one at a time. This way, you will have to blame your horse if you die on the end of that rope.'

'Who are you?' Breed wanted to know.

'I'm a Valeron, boys,' he answered quietly. 'And we Valerons believe in justice.'

'You going to leave us here until our horses decide to walk away?' Kidd asked.

'No, I'm taking you to Denver. The ones who hired you should be in custody by this time. I'm sure it'll be like a family reunion for you.'

Breed opened his mouth to speak, but his horse leaned down and snatched a bit of grass.

'Whoa!' he said with some anxiety. 'Steady, girl.'

Jared gave their dire situation a grave once-over and shook his head. 'Gilding and a mare – hope they get along all right. Be your tough luck if anything should spook them.'

'Listen, Valeron,' Kidd pleaded. 'We've got several hundred dollars between us. It's yours if you let us go!'

'Keep your voice down,' Valeron warned. 'Your nag's ears just flattened out. You know that's never a good sign.'

'Uh, easy, fella,' Kidd coaxed, trying to rub the horse with the bound hands behind his back. 'Nice, boy.'

'I'll tell you what I told Kidd,' Jared spoke to Breed. 'If one of you decides to yell or shout to warn your wounded pal, these two animals would likely react – maybe move or jump from the noise. It could be the last mistake of your lives. Tight as those nooses are, you don't have any room for a fidgeting pony.'

Both men remained silent, other than for trying to keep their horse calm. Jared grinned at their grim acceptance of the situation and moved easily back a few steps. Two down and one to go.

Nash was up early to see Martin and Wendy off. It came as no surprise that Trina was there also. Dutch had the wagon ready for them and there was little time for good-byes. Reb and Dodge came from the bunkhouse in time to also bid them farewell.

Any hopes Trina had about catching Nash alone was crushed. Dodge rode out with the two ranch hands, but Reb was going to finish some of the bookkeeping that Martin had lined out. They hoped to finish the tally on the number of cattle by the end of the day.

After breakfast, Reb took to the books and Nash sat at his side, computing figures and finishing what Martin had started. It was mid-morning when the two of them relaxed from their efforts.

'Looks as if the ranch is in pretty good shape,' Reb remarked to Nash. 'I haven't done much of this here bookkeeping since me and Dodge had our own ranch.' He laughed. 'By jingo! That was a long time back. Didn't even get through the second year before we went belly-up.'

'Hard to start a ranch on a shoestring,' Nash sympathized. 'Pa, Temple and Udall had a rough go of it for the first few years too.'

'I remember,' Reb said. 'We were among the first full-time hands they hired.'

'You've been like family,' Nash said. 'I remember you teaching Shane to ride a horse.'

Reb laughed. 'A week later, that young broncobuster was riding anything on four legs. Never seen anyone take to horseback any quicker than him.'

'How come you turned down the foreman's job when Pa offered it to you?' Nash asked him. 'You've always been good with figures, and could have easily done the payroll and such.'

'Dodge never learnt how to read,' Reb replied. 'Me and him have been like brothers since the War.

143

Wouldn't seem right, me having a cushy job, earning more money than him, let alone telling him what to do. Ain't a man in the country got more savvy about cattle than Dodge.'

Trina had been in the next room, sorting through her father's belongings and converting it into her bedroom. She had not intended to eavesdrop, but she heard every word exchanged between Nash and Reb. Some of the tidbits of information rattled around in her head, like an idea that hadn't quite formed, but was right near the surface of her consciousness.

Impulsively, she removed the piece of paper Wendy had given her. She knew exactly what was written on it, but she read over it again and again.

Maybe . . . she thought. *It's a ridiculous idea, but it just might work!*

Lobo opened his eyes and saw a man standing over him. He blinked in confusion and grabbed for his gun!

The holster was empty.

'Howdy!' Jared greeted him with a smile . . . and a Colt pointed at his nose. 'Nice day for a hanging.'

Lobo swore under his breath, and warily rose to a sitting position. His head jerked around, looking for Breed and Kidd.

'What's the idea, mister?'

'Put your boots on and let's go see if your partners are still waiting for you.' Jared added a look of concern. 'They seemed real eager for me to wake you, but I'm a soft-hearted sort, so I let you sleep.'

As soon as Lobo was on his feet, Jared bound his

hands behind his back with a strip of rawhide. They marched out of camp, past the one remaining horse, and down to a large tree.

Lobo spotted the two men, with ropes about their necks, sitting atop the two horses. He stopped in his tracks and threw a wild look over his shoulder at Jared.

'What the. . . ?' he began. 'What are you doing?'

'Sh-h-h!' Jared warned him. 'You'll frighten the horses.'

But seeing Jared reminded the horses of the oats he had hand-fed them during the night. One of the animals started forward, wanting another taste. Not to miss out on the treat, the second horse also walked towards Jared. The result of their movement unseated both riders.

'Holy hell!' Lobo wailed loudly. 'You've hanged them!'

Jared tripped and shoved Lobo to the ground. He pulled his skinning knife and hurried past the two horses, then pushed by the dangling and kicking men. With a swipe of his blade, he rapidly cut through the ropes that held the two men aloft. Soon as they hit the ground, he took a moment to loosen their nooses.

Breed and Kidd gasped for air, cursing the rope burn around their necks, and venting their wrath at Jared. He ignored their complaints, put away his knife, and took time to herd Lobo over to join them.

'That was pretty close, eh, fellas?' Jared joked. 'If I'd have been another couple steps away, you would be swapping lies with the devil about now.'

'Real funny!' Breed snarled his displeasure. 'You

145

about kilt us both!'

Jared gave him a sharp look. 'Better be glad you were carrying lariats on your saddles, my friend. I'll be switched if I would have cut my own rope just to save your worthless necks.'

'What you gonna do with us now?' Kidd wanted to know.

'It's like I told you, we're all going to Denver. You get to face the charges from your wanted posters and confess about trying to kill us. If the judge is one of them benevolent, forgiving sorts, you might only get twenty years in the state prison.'

Jared let the three of them stew about their future while he saddled the horses. He put all three animals on lead ropes, one strung to the next – bridle to saddle. Then he used the same technique with the remaining lariat, securing it from his saddle to each man's neck, one behind the other. There would be no trying to use a horse or diversion to attempt an escape. If one man broke the line or fell off, they would all end up either strangled by the rope or with broken necks.

As the small procession started down the trail, Breed bellowed at Jared, 'You can't watch all of us all of the time,' he avowed. 'It's sixty miles or more to Denver from here. We won't make that in one day, not in this rough terrain.'

'Breed,' Jared replied over his shoulder, 'threats like that tend to make me right skittish. Want to know what happens if I can't stay awake or think you might jump me?'

'Tell me . . . what?'

He rotated in the saddle, pointed an index finger at him, with his thumb in the air. He made a gesture of pulling the trigger, his thumb dropping like the hammer of a gun.

'Think about it, stupid,' he jeered. 'I get too tired, I will shoot each of you before I throw down a blanket and take a nap. When I wake up refreshed, I'll drape you over your horses. Dead bodies are much easier to transport than live ones.' He displayed a sadistic grin. 'And the upside is, I get paid the bounty on you either way!'

A twisted snarl came to Breed's lips, but he didn't speak again. None of them did.

Dutch came to the house and informed Nash that one of their riders had sprained or broken his wrist. Nash took his medical bag and tended to the man out at the bunkhouse. It turned out to be a simple sprain, but he wrapped it snug enough for support and told him to do the same for the next few days. If he babied it some, it would heal in a couple weeks.

He was surprised when he returned to the house. Reb had left the bookkeeping, opting to take a ride and check on the cattle counting with Dodge. Mildred met him at the porch, dressed for a trip to town, with a list of items in her hand.

'Dutch is getting the runabout,' she told him. 'With so many extra mouths to feed, I'm running short of supplies.'

'Do you need me to drive you?' he asked.

'No,' she said with a smile. 'Dutch has been taking

me in to do the weekly shopping ever since I came to work. We have an enjoyable ride together.'

'OK,' he replied.

'But,' she added, 'I left some beans and ham warming on the stove. Miss Barrett said she would serve it up for lunch. I should be back in time to prepare supper . . . though it might be a little later than usual.'

'You are a blessing here on the ranch, ma'am.'

She beamed at his flattery, but then grew serious. 'Oh, I wanted to tell you ...' lowering her voice, 'something in private.'

'Yes, what is it?'

'I think Miss Barrett is feeling rather poorly. She was complaining of chest pains and is lying down on her bed.' She gave him a worried look. 'I wonder if you'd look in on her?'

'Chest pains can be serious,' Nash surmised. 'I'll visit her straightaway.'

'Please do. She seems like a wonderful girl.'

He already had his medical bag, so he bid her goodbye and wished her and Dutch a safe journey. Then he hurried through the house. He paused before entering Trina's bedroom.

'Miss Barrett?' he queried. 'May I come in?'

'Oh, please!' Her voice sounded strangely constricted. 'You needn't bother. I'm fine.'

Nash pushed open the door. The window cast adequate light for him to see the young woman. Trina was wearing a white dressing gown and stretched out on top of the covers. Her honey blonde hair was decorated loosely about the pillow, accenting her fair complexion and delicate features. As he approached, he perceived tears at the surface of her eyes. Drawing near, he observed her face was flushed, and she appeared to be trembling.

'Trina!' he exclaimed, kneeling down at her bedside. 'My dear, sweet girl! Whatever is the matter? Tell me! Where does it hurt?'

She swallowed hard, as if it was difficult to speak. 'It's' – she whispered softly – 'it's here in my chest.'

He fearfully opened his bag. 'Why didn't you say something? How long have you had these pains?'

She rose up onto her elbows and reached out with a restraining hand, catching hold of his wrist. 'There's nothing in your black bag that will help.'

He gave her a perplexed stare. 'What do you mean?'

Trina remained on her elbows. As she looked at him, her features softened. 'I believe it's my heart,' she said gravely.

'Your heart?'

Demurely, 'Yes.'

Nash was speechless and wholly confused.

She lowered the lashes of her eyes, as if embarrassed to meet his inquisitive scrutiny. 'If you leave me' – she murmured – 'it will surely break.'

Nash remained on his knees, but sat back on his heels at her confession. 'But . . . b-but the ranch,' he stammered. 'This is what you wanted! It's why we all pitched in to help, so you could get back your ranch!'

'No,' she corrected him. 'It was my freedom I wanted back. Since I met you, worked with you—' The tears readily spilled down her cheeks. 'Nash,' she managed

149

weakly, barely uttering the words, 'I want to spend my life with you – as your nurse . . . your confidant . . . your wife.'

A tidal wave of emotion swept over Nash, drowning his senses in wonder, awe and affection. His voice had no response – words could not express his feelings. Leaning forward, he gently placed his lips on hers. When she slipped her arms around his neck, he knew he'd found the woman he would live with, love with, and grow old with.

CHAPTER ELEVEN

Robby topped the crest of the hill and stared at the most bizarre sight in his life. A lone rider was leading three other men on horseback, each of them linked to the next by a rope from one man's neck to the other.

He neck-reined his horse quickly to cover behind a sprawling piñon and continued to watch. Within moments, he recognized the captured men as Breed, Kidd and Lobo. The man in front had to be a Valeron. No one else in this part of the country would dare try to bring in three deadly outlaws all by himself.

'Is that you, Wyatt?' Robby snickered. 'What an unholy terror you must be, to have captured Breed and the others all by yourself.'

Taking a gander about, he saw the path being taken by the four mounted horsemen was the same trail he had been riding. With higher, choppy hills and low mountains running to either side, this was the best route to Denver or his ranch. He found a good spot to hide his horse and tied him off. Then he sneaked down the hill until he reached a good place from which to surprise Valeron.

Robby's mind was working as he waited. This was the best scenario he could have hoped for. Breed and the others would be beholden to him for saving their hides. Robby wouldn't have to pay Breed the balance of their deal. All he needed to do was sit back and wait for his mother to contact him. Without these men to testify, who would point a finger at either him or her?

After all, James Barrett's death was thought to have been a heart attack. And Trina had been lawfully confined in the asylum, using the legal process of a hearing to determine her mental wellness. The doctor might be in trouble, if proof could be produced that he had been controlling his patients with medication, but his mother could avoid any blame. She was smart and cunning, and the lawyer representing her would be the same one who helped put Trina away. So what, if Trina got back the ranch? He and his mother would have $2,000 to start a new business – something without a lot of cows or long hours!

He began to hum softly. Yes, sir, things were all coming his way, starting with the biggest dog in the woods – Valeron!

Weariness had beaten down Jared until his shoulders sagged under the weight of the late-afternoon sun. He was dirty, hungry, unshaven, and desperate for sleep. He had hoped to reach Denver by midnight, but there was little chance of that. The mountainous region ahead was slow going. And, in spite of his grit and boasting, he didn't relish the idea of trying to keep watch over three desperate killers all night.

He glanced back at the string of animals and saw they were dragging their feet too. They needed food and rest or they might not all complete the journey. He shouldn't have been so adamant about tracking the three men alone. True, he was much better on his own, but there were times when—

'That's far enough!' a man's voice commanded, as he stepped out from behind a stand of boulders. A rifle was in his hands, with the muzzle pointed right at Jared's chest.

Jared stopped and the parade following did the same. Looking at the rifleman, Jared knew he had no chance to draw his weapon. For one thing, the leather thong was hooked over the hammer of his gun, to keep it from slipping from the holster. As the gun directed at him was likely cocked and ready to fire, it would have been futile to attempt a fight.

'Howdy!' Jared said, flashing his teeth in a smile. 'What's your problem, friend?'

The fellow shook his head. 'I'm not your friend, Valeron.'

'Hey! Boys!' Breed called to his two companions. 'It's Robby!'

Both of them let out a shout of joy.

'Whadda you think, Breed?' Robby asked the gang leader. 'You want the pleasure of killing this *hombre*?'

'Best think twice about shooting me,' Jared warned. 'If a gun goes off, my horse will react and the other three will also spook. You are liable to rescue three dead men. No way the short little train behind me stays put.'

Robby had to consider the situation. With ropes around their necks, only one of the mounts had to shy or balk at a gunshot. If one man was jerked from his saddle, it would mean death to all three of them.

Robby began to sidestep, making an effort to get in front of Jared's horse. He figured to be in a position to grab his steed and prevent the other horses from breaking away. After his second step, Jared touched the neck of his horse, causing it to turn in the direction of the hillside. It was quite steep, with loose shale rock and dirt at that point, so the animal would not get much traction and would likely do a lot of slipping and sliding. That much really wouldn't matter, because any sudden movement should unseat a rider or two.

'Stand still!' the young man warned.

'You move . . . I move,' Jared told him. 'We have us a stand-off, because I won't let you walk up and grab the reins of my horse. You get too close, I dig in my heels and your three pals will wind up being dragged along the ground by their necks!'

Robby grew frustrated. 'Breed! What'll I do?'

The leader of the band grunted. 'Shoot him, Robby. Kill the dirty son, then grab the nearest horse. Even if one of us is pulled off, you ought to be able to snake the noose from our necks before we strangle to death.'

'Breed's right,' Lobo seconded the motion. 'Kill Valeron . . . and to hell with what happens next!'

Robby threw the rifle to his shoulder to aim and fire.

Jared dug his heels into his mare. As she jumped, a rifle shot sounded—

154

As the string of animals were severely jaded and glad for a moment's rest, they weren't ready for a sudden start. His horse only took one lunge, then about fell down from lack of footing and the tautness from the lead rope from the other three ponies holding her back. Jared was stunned. Robby had somehow missed him! He clawed loose his pistol and swung around in the saddle—

But Robby was on his knees, the rifle barrel jammed into the dirt in front of him. His eyes were wide with shock and horror, as blood spread a dark blotch on his shirtfront. His head turned back and forth in disbelief. With a painful grimace on his face, he opened his mouth to question what had happened. No words came forth and he pitched forward onto his face.

Jared searched up the hillside and spotted Wyatt Valeron, standing just below the hill's summit with a rifle in his hand. He waved, then disappeared to get his horse. A minute later, he came riding down to where Jared was still sitting his horse.

'What say, cuz?' he grinned. 'You aren't the only one who can handle a rifle.'

'At less than a hundred yards away?' he scoffed. 'Shucks, Wendy could have hit Robby from there.'

Wyatt laughed, then looked at the three bound men. 'What's the deal, Jerry? I see you have three prisoners . . . all of them still kicking!'

'You notice they have ropes around their necks,' Jared replied. 'They are trying them on for size.'

'I think you must be getting soft in your old age.'

'More careless, that's for sure. Awake a mere thirty

hours or so and I walked right into an ambush.'

'Yes, but bringing the gang in alive? It's going to ruin your reputation.'

Jared chortled. 'Well, I actually did hang two of them, but it didn't take.'

The surreal statement caused a wrinkle in Wyatt's brow. 'Hard to believe,' he said, 'after all of the practice you've had.'

'I'm beholden to you for saving my can,' Jared thanked him, offering no further explanation. 'I didn't see any way out for me, other than trying to take Breed and his two men with me.'

'You can owe me one,' Wyatt joked. Getting back to their situation, he suggested, 'I crossed a nice little stream a few hours back. We can make an early camp there for the night and rest your horses and your old bones.'

'I'm only one year your senior, Wyatt,' Jared complained. 'So, let's knock off the getting old remarks.'

'Get started, cuz. I'll load Robby over his horse and catch up before you get very far.'

Jared paused and formed a serious expression. 'Thanks again, Wyatt. I mean it.'

'We both know you'd have done the same . . .' with a grin, 'only you'd have shot him from a lot farther away, just to make the story sound better when you started bragging to the family.'

Jared laughed, then turned his horse back to the main trail. As Wyatt rounded up Robby's horse, he started his string moving.

It was late afternoon the following day when Jared and Wyatt arrived at the Barrett ranch house. They had four horses in tow. Nash and Reb came out to greet them, and Dutch wandered over from the corral to help with the livestock.

'What's with all the extra horses?' Nash asked.

'The boys riding these broncs won't be needing them any longer,' Jared told his brother. 'Martin gone?'

'He and Wendy left the day after we arrived.'

Jared grinned. 'Guess I'll have to put off teasing her until we get home.'

'Don't you dare!' Trina spoke from the doorway. 'Your sister took up for me at Nash's office! She is the one who saved me from being returned to that horrible asylum.'

Jared rubbed his chin. 'Seems to me I had a piece of that action too.'

Trina showed a ready smile. 'Yes, but you were standing up for your sister. She was standing up for me.'

'What you have to understand, Miss Barrett,' Wyatt put in, 'is that Wendy would think she had done something to hurt Jared's feelings if he didn't give her a hard time. Besides,' he clarified further, 'when it comes to sass or teasing, Wendy can hold her own with anyone on the ranch.'

'It's why we call her *Wendy*,' Jared said.

'Yes, I know the story.'

'Were you told or did you guess?' Wyatt asked.

Trina smiled at his humor and invited the two Valeron arrivals inside. 'Dutch can put up the horses.'

'It's my job,' the man said. 'And I'll take no backtalk

from either of you. Way I see it, I owe you boys a real debt. Whilst Lucile and her rotten offspring were running things, I was about one weak moment away from killing them in their sleep. Worst people I ever worked for.'

Jared and Wyatt turned over the reins and lead rope from the animals. Jared took a moment to retrieve one of the saddle-bags, before the two of them brushed the dust off their hats and entered the house.

Trina asked Mildred if she would kindly add two more for the supper table, then went in to the sitting room. She sat next to Nash – close enough that Wyatt dug an elbow into Jared's ribs. The two exchanged grins, but said nothing.

When everyone was seated, Nash outlined what was painfully obvious to the newcomers.

'There's been a slight change in plans, since I last spoke to you,' he began. 'Dodge and Reb are going to stick here and run the ranch. Reb knows the accounting, payroll and such; Dodge will ramrod the rest of the place. They will take care of the hired hands, cattle drives and keep the ranch solvent. Each year, if there is a profit, it will be split between the three of them – Dodge, Reb and Trina.'

'Looks like we will need to hire a couple of good men,' Jared commented. 'You just stole the best we had on the Valeron ranch.'

'They were due a promotion,' Nash countered.

'Plus,' Reb interjected, 'me and Dodge are slowing down. Neither of us can handle sleeping on the ground any more. This here management job will allow us to spend the nights here in the house. Having a man to tend the animals and run the yard, plus a live-in house-keeper and cook . . . it'll be almost like being retired.'

'Guess we don't have to ask what Miss Barrett has lined out for her future,' Jared said with a smirk. 'Can't fit a slip of paper betwixt the two of you. When's the wedding?'

Trina blushed and Nash uttered a nervous laugh. 'Well, Jerry, we haven't set a date yet. We wanted to get the building finished in Castle Point, so we would have enough rooms for more than one patient at a time.'

'Or a child or two added to the family,' Wyatt added.

That brought some laughter, but Reb broke it up by asking, 'So what about them ambushers? And what about Robby?'

'Here's the money from the sale of your cattle,' Jared spoke to Trina. 'I reckon that will help catch up some bills around the place.'

'You. . . .' She gave her head a negative shake. 'I can't begin to thank you!' Looking at Wyatt, 'All of you!'

'The three bushwhackers are in jail,' Jared outlined, 'you got your money back, plus a reward is being sent to Nash, up at Castle Point. As for Robby, he has a reservation at a Denver boneyard.'

'Jared, old son,' Reb did not hide his amazement, 'I can't believe you done brung them back-shooters in alive.'

'Well,' Jared told him, 'I hanged a couple of them for a few seconds, but my conscience got the best of me. I thought I'd let the Denver lawmen do it up proper.'

'And Robby?' he queried. 'How'd he end up dead?'

'He was about to—' Wyatt began.

'Killed when he tried to ambush me,' Jared talked over any details. 'Man should have known better than to mess with a Valeron.' Then he quickly asked, 'How about the old hag and the crooked doctor?'

'Both in jail for murder,' Nash informed them. 'Dizzy and Wendy put their heads together and figured a way to give him a dose of his own medicine. The blubbering fool confessed in court!'

'Reckon that wraps up everything in a Christmas bow,' Wyatt congratulated everyone involved.

Jared grinned. 'At least, until the wedding.' He offered a salacious wink at Trina. 'I'm already looking forward to kissing the bride!'

Nash gave him a sharp look. 'Don't get your hopes up, big brother. A kiss from anyone but me will be on Trina's cheek!'

Wyatt smiled at Trina. 'Welcome to the family, Trina. For better and for worse, you'll soon be one of the Valerons.'